Praise for Francesca Marciano's

ANIMAL SPIRIT

"With this collection of radiant short stories set mostly in Rome, Marciano claims a spot beside the best practitioners of the form. . . . Marciano's characters tread gingerly across emotional minefields, 'kaleidoscopically vulnerable' amid the piazze and palazzi of the Eternal City. Creatures of all kinds—a beguiling stray pup, Hitchcockian seagulls—guide them toward keener understandings of their own desires."
—*O, The Oprah Magazine*

"This short story collection erupts from Francesca Marciano's head like Athena sprang from Zeus's, its tales both measured and erotic, and filled with predators and creatures and worrisome thoughts. . . . Marciano's human characters, mainly women, are interrupted, obsessed, created, falling apart, in search of something, and their stories contain as many layers as Rome's streets, pressed deliciously together, all sitting on top of history itself. . . . Nothing is as tame as we think, including our own sense of control."   —Literary Hub

"Really satisfying. . . . Exotic settings, wild animals, Italian details—thank you, Francesca Marciano."
—Baltimore Public Radio

"[*Animal Spirit*] surprised me with its power. . . . [Marciano] is such a clear-eyed writer, showing with particular skill and compassion what makes her characters tick. . . . [*Animal Spirit* is], in truth, about us—about all of the lovely and terrible things that make us human."

—Ashley Riggleson, *The Free Lance-Star*

"Marciano displays a spellbinding sense of control over her characters, and she does so with surprising brevity and well-composed pacing. . . . There's a sense of confidence in each sentence that allows the reader to be as vulnerable as her characters. . . . A passionate, compelling exercise in the fine art of short fiction. It's proof that the most intimate narratives are often the most powerful."

—*BookPage*

"Marciano is a master at making even the most seemingly banal settings seem forbiddingly foreign . . . and she excels at crafting conclusions that are both satisfying and enigmatic."

—*Booklist*

"[A] sharp-eyed and effortlessly graceful collection, . . . set largely in the author's native Italy, explores the ways people's animalistic instincts drive relationships. . . . Polished and compulsively readable, this is a real treat."

—*Publishers Weekly* (starred review)

"Vibrantly described. . . . Rich, leisurely. . . . Death's lasting power echoes back through the stories, but Marciano's closing lines offer hard-won hope. Emotionally charged issues of commitment, loyalty, and trust explored with dry yet oddly comforting European wit." —*Kirkus Reviews* (starred review)

Francesca Marciano

ANIMAL SPIRIT

Francesca Marciano is the author of the novels *Rules of the Wild*, *Casa Rossa*, and *The End of Manners*, and the story collection *The Other Language*. She lives in Rome.

ANIMAL SPIRIT

ANIMAL SPIRIT

Stories

Francesca Marciano

———

Vintage Contemporaries

VINTAGE BOOKS

A DIVISION OF PENGUIN RANDOM HOUSE LLC

NEW YORK

FIRST VINTAGE CONTEMPORARIES EDITION, MAY 2021

Copyright © 2020 by Francesca Marciano

The Library of Congress has cataloged the Pantheon edition as follows:
Name: Marciano, Francesca, author.
Title: Animal spirit : stories / Francesca Marciano.
Description: First edition. | New York : Pantheon Books, 2020.
Identifiers: LCCN 2019041662
Classification: LCC PR9120.9.M36 A6 2020 | DDC 823/.914—dc23
LC record available at https://lccn.loc.gov/2019041662

Vintage Contemporaries Trade Paperback ISBN: 978-0-525-56574-1
eBook ISBN: 978-1-5247-4816-6

Book design by Anna B. Knighton

www.vintagebooks.com

CONTENTS

ANIMAL SPIRIT

TERRIBLE THINGS
COULD HAPPEN TO US

Sandro felt the phone purring inside his pocket. It was a few minutes past eight in the evening, an odd time for Emilia to be calling him. Usually by then she was busy making dinner for her family.

"He's dead," she said.

Her voice on speakerphone resonated loudly inside the taxi. Lately Sandro had been trying to keep his cell as far as possible from his ear, fearing radiation and a potential brain tumor. He immediately switched the speaker off, lifted the phone to his ear and lowered his voice, sensing tension in the shoulders of the cabdriver, as if he too were eager to hear the details.

"Dead? Who?"

"Bruno. He's had a stroke, a heart attack . . . not sure yet what, exactly. He was driving home from work, he lost control of the car, apparently he managed to pull onto the side of the road and . . ."

Her voice trembled.

"Oh God, I can't believe I'm telling you this—it feels so unreal. He died on the spot."

"When?" he asked, as if it made any difference, but he needed a few seconds to take it all in.

"Like . . . an hour ago. I'm at the hospital now."

"Do you . . . I mean . . . do you want me to come over? I'm on my way to something but I can make up an excuse."

"No, I don't think it would be a good idea. His sisters are here, and my friend Monica from the yoga studio is on her way."

"What about the girls?"

"My mother is at home with them. I haven't told them anything yet."

There was a pause. He could hear her anxious breathing.

"This is so . . ." He hesitated. "*Amore,* this is . . . I'm really sorry. I wish I could do something for you right now."

"I know, I know." She was crying. "But it's good to hear your voice; it makes me feel less lonely."

He lowered his voice to a whisper.

"I wish I could hold you in my arms."

"Me too," she murmured. "I so wish you were here with me, but it's not possible—that's crazy, isn't it. I can barely think straight right now."

"I know, of course."

The driver turned toward him.

"Is this it?"

The cab had slowed down, skirting the museum of contemporary art, a grandiose building that resembled a whale. The MAXXI had cost millions of euros yet some people said it wasn't art-friendly; the interior had way too many curves and spirals and basically there weren't enough walls to hang paintings on.

"Yes, yes. We can stop here," Sandro said, checking his wallet for small bills.

"Can I call you later—is that all right?" Emilia asked, trying to conceal her sobs.

"Of course. Send me a text and I'll call you right back. I love you," he said.

He felt terrible, to be going to a stupid opening and leaving Emilia alone in the midst of her tragedy.

He wiped his forehead with a handkerchief—it was an unusually warm evening for early May—and regretted his decision to wear a jacket, even though it was a light linen one.

Sandro walked across the courtyard, where a gigantic sculpture had been placed, probably the work of the Korean artist whose vernissage he was attending. It was an enormous oval, reminiscent of an alien ship from outer space, or maybe a dinosaur's egg. Its surface was beautifully polished, perfectly smooth; it looked peaceful and strangely benign.

Sandro couldn't care less about contemporary art—he knew next to nothing about who was who in that world—but his wife, Ottavia, came from a family of important collectors; she had grown up surrounded by artists and had just opened a gallery herself. This was her scene, and he knew how much it meant to her to have him by her side at these kinds of events.

He's dead. As he approached the sliding door of the museum, Sandro kept repeating the words to himself, in an attempt to make the concept real before he stepped inside. He could see the usual crowd through the glass, milling around in the lobby, champagne flutes in hand, air-kissing and Instagramming.

So it had happened at last. He had often entertained this fantasy. It would come out of nowhere, against his will, but he would frequently think how perfect it would be if Emilia's husband suddenly died, or Ottavia, or both. He felt guilty to be imagining this scenario, but who in his position wouldn't think of the possibility? He and Emilia had fallen in love almost a year earlier, and the death of their spouses seemed the only way to set them free. What if they just disappeared, without suffering, just like that, at the drop of a hat?

And now it had happened, and he wasn't sure how he felt.

He caught a glimpse of his wife standing next to the recently appointed curator of the museum—a young woman with short platinum hair and an elaborate tattoo on her shoulder blades, two bright blue hummingbirds facing each other. Things had changed recently in the art world, Ottavia had explained to him. It was the very young, the very cool and the women who had the power now.

"Sandro!" His wife moved away from the tattooed curator and kissed him lightly on the cheek. A vintage yellow dress looked great against her tanned skin, along with a turquoise Navajo bracelet on each wrist. She wasn't fearful of bold colors. He was suddenly overwhelmed by the reality of her body next to his, her scent, the warmth of her skin. He grabbed her hand and clutched it in his. Ottavia looked surprised.

"What?"

"Nothing. You look beautiful. I love this dress—you should wear it more often."

Sandro couldn't believe he'd say something so trivial, but it helped him feel anchored to reality.

"Thank you, darling. The show is a joke, but we need to stay till the bitter end. Are you going to be able to bear the dinner afterward?"

"Of course," he said, and smiled at his beautiful wife, the

mother of his daughter, Ilaria. Ottavia, whom he had wished dead more than once.

"Let's go get a drink," he said. He put his arm around her and they moved toward the bar. As they walked, he pressed his fingertips along her spine, feeling the tiny interstices between each vertebra, the evidence that underneath that delicate flesh lived a skeleton. We are all so frail, he thought. Terrible things could happen to us in the space of one breath.

———

Emilia's girls could not at all take in the fact that their father had vanished like that. One moment he was on the phone asking what they wanted for a pizza he'd bring home in ten minutes—Napoli for Emilia and Capricciosa for Anita and Sofia—and the next he was dead. Someone had found the pizza boxes piled in the passenger seat of his car, still warm. They were children without any means of processing their first encounter with death. Even after two full days of learning that Bruno was not going to come back and take them to school in his Volvo or pick them up from swimming lessons or cook *pollo alla cacciatora* on Sunday, they were unable to cry. They refused to believe they were never going to see him again. Rather than a tragedy, his death felt to them like a magician's trick, and they were waiting for someone to come and undo it.

Because no one in the family was a believer, and Bruno's fervent Catholic parents had both passed away, Emilia had organized a nonreligious service. The girls were disappointed. Anita was almost twelve and Sofia only eight, both ages where children still may not be ready yet to proclaim themselves atheists. A ceremony in a church filled with flowers, incense and organ music had seemed the least their mother would want for their father, but Emilia explained that Bruno had been a very coherent man when it came to political and philosophical principles and he would have strongly opposed having a priest give him his last farewell. Emilia further explained that she and their father once had had a conversation about the eventuality of one of them dying (she refrained from saying they'd been high on a joint and gotten carried away describing in detail what kind of service the other one had to organize, just in case). Bruno told her he wanted a memorial with all of his friends in the cemetery in Testaccio, a non-Catholic site otherwise known as the Englishmen's Cemetery, where Keats and Shelley were buried along with Gregory Corso and Antonio Gramsci. He also mentioned they should play "Space Oddity" by David Bowie at the very end.

People crowded the small nondenominational chapel, where Bruno's friends, siblings—two sisters and one brother—cousins and work colleagues each took a turn giving a speech, provoking laughter and tears, reminiscing about legendary episodes in which Bruno was the intrepid protagonist: the dress-up party where he showed up in the most elaborate outfit as Queen Elizabeth I; the full moon night, when, drunk, he decided he was going to climb a mountain in Spain and actually got to the top without any gear; or how he was able to recite more than fifty verses of *The Odyssey* in classical Greek. Hearing these stories for the first time made the girls feel even closer to the father they had just lost. They could picture him younger, funny and absurd. Yes, he had been reckless and daring in his younger days, yet everyone agreed on one thing: Bruno had been the sweetest, most loyal, most generous person they'd ever met. A man with principles, integrity, a great sense of humor. And what a great father he'd been, so in love with his girls. During these testimonials the girls felt soothed by the warmth of so many people who had loved Bruno. They felt, if only in that moment, that they were not alone, but instead had just acquired a new, larger family of adults. As they exited the chapel, blinded by the midday blaring light, they managed to cry at last, buoyed by the momentum the drums and vocals of "Space Oddity" provided.

After the service, the apartment filled up with people. It's important, their only grandmother left was telling them, to share a meal after someone dies; friends and neighbors are supposed to take care of the family and put food on the table.

Amid the heat and the confusion created by grown-ups who had cried and drunk too much, who kept hugging one another while eating out of paper plates, dropping cold couscous on the floor, they spotted a stranger. Anita and Sofia had never seen Sandro before. He was handsome, very formal in his gray suit, unlike any other of their parents' friends. He looked like a lawyer, or maybe a businessman, but more than anything, he looked rich. Richer than any of the people who had ever come to cook and eat with them.

Sandro looked uneasy, as though he didn't know what to do with himself. He wasn't eating or drinking, and he didn't seem to know anybody in the room. He just stood silently against the wall, darting quick glances now and then toward Emilia, who was going back and forth from the kitchen, picking up plates, chatting to guests, nervous and distracted.

Anita had noticed how, among all those tears and celebrations, her mother was the only one who hadn't made a speech.

It was understandable in a way, but she worried that Emilia wasn't looking sufficiently heartbroken after losing her own husband.

Anita remembered her parents being happy up until a couple of years before, when she was still in elementary school. Whenever they could—in the car, on the street or on the couch—they would be touching or holding each other. They kissed in the strange way people did in films, with their mouths half open, doing something with their tongues (what exactly was going on when adults kissed like that, she wasn't sure, but she knew it meant they were in love). Then something had changed—they no longer tongue-kissed, there was less touching, less laughing, they both seemed more serious and often in a strange mood. If their bedroom door was closed she could hear their low voices seep through, cutting each other off, rushing and gurgling like a torrent. What was so important to discuss for that long? Why did they have to do it behind doors? She worried, because although she couldn't make out the words, their voices sounded so grave.

Sofia appeared at her side, looking pale and sweaty, her damp curls stuck to her temples. She pointed her chin toward Sandro, who was standing by the door across the room.

"Who is he?"

"I don't know," Anita said.

The sisters watched Emilia move toward him. The two of them cautiously exchanged quick words, like people sharing a secret.

"Is he a friend of Papà's?"

"No. I think he's Mamma's new friend," Anita said, with a tinge of sarcasm.

Sofia swiftly turned her head, frightened. Was she joking?

"I'm kidding. He's probably someone from the yoga studio," Anita quickly reassured her.

Slowly, as evening came, people began to gather their things and get ready to leave. Everyone looked exhausted, as if they'd run a marathon, and they hugged the girls, holding them a tad too long and tighter than necessary. Only Bruno's sisters and a few close friends were left. They sat on the couch around Emilia or on the floor, and spoke in lazy tones among themselves. Someone picked up Bruno's acoustic guitar and played a wistful song. The house felt peaceful again, and the cat felt it was safe to come out of his hiding spot and jump in Emilia's lap. Around nine o'clock the girls decided it was a good time to go back to their room. They changed into their nightgowns and brushed their teeth, hoping that by going through their daily motions they could gain some relief. They got into bed. Anita picked up her book, and after a few minutes Sofia did the same. They read in silence, although they struggled to concentrate. They had no words to define how they felt and what they were afraid of, even though they sensed there were reasons to be afraid of what was coming. For now, it seemed possible to rest, and let the voices of the women in the living room lull them into sleep.

Anita woke up with a start. The luminous clock on her bedside table said 11:52. She heard voices coming from the living room. She scuttled out of bed and walked slowly out to the corridor. It was dark, but a blade of light seeped through the half-closed door of the living room. Peeking through a crack, she had a good view of the sofa. Her mother and Sandro were facing each other at each end of the couch. Emilia had stretched her legs so that her bare feet touched his knees; Sandro had taken off his jacket and rolled up the sleeves of his white shirt. He must've come back, maybe after everyone else had left, Anita thought. She watched him pour two drinks from a bottle of Scotch she'd never before seen in the house. She could hear the ice clinking and cracking in the tall glasses.

And they were laughing.

———

Ottavia knew, of course. But her strategy so far had been to pretend she didn't.

She was born into a family where certain things weren't ever questioned. Her mother had been a stoic example, a tall, severe ash-blonde who'd lived all her life with a serial philanderer. *Husband and wife stay together no matter what,* was her credo; there was too much at stake in a good marriage. Too much shared history: children, of course, but also money and properties, plus certain privileges and connections that being a couple provided, all of which would be utterly foolish to give up. It was only a matter of waiting: after all, men fell in lust and, with time, lust evaporated. The secret was to be patient till the crush wore out. Meanwhile, it was crucial to avoid any confrontation. Eventually they all came back home.

"You don't want to find out her name, where she lives, what she does," her mother lectured her, glancing at the menu.

They were having lunch at their favorite Japanese restaurant near the Pantheon and Ottavia had just mentioned her suspicion that Sandro might be having an affair. He was distracted, vague about his movements, too often away or late at work.

"It's toxic." Her mother sipped her jasmine tea from a tiny

handmade ceramic cup. "The minute you know who she is, it all becomes real and the obsession takes hold of you. Once the monster is out of the box, you won't be able to get rid of it. You will start stalking her, checking his messages and turn into a policeman, which is the worst thing you can do to your marriage. Better to just sit in a limbo, the foggier the better, and be as nice as possible. I promise you, it's like a fever that has to run its course."

Ottavia wasn't convinced.

"You make it sound so easy."

"It's probably some young sexy intern at the office," her mother said with a disparaging tone.

"They're not his type. He's not that kind."

"Don't be so sure," the mother said, turning her ring around her finger. "It's typical of a midlife crisis. He's what now, forty-one, forty-two?"

Ottavia raised her eyebrow. "Okay, can we please change the subject now?" Ottavia said. "I can't be hearing any more about this from you, okay?"

Ottavia was good-looking and still in perfect shape at thirty-five. She had sworn she would try to age gracefully and not do anything to her face. She had a master's in medieval history, was a successful art dealer who was well known internationally, came from money and was making quite a bit on her own. She was considered engaging and intelligent. The idea that her husband was cheating on her seemed inexplicable. What did this other woman have that she didn't?

She had inherited some of the cynical wisdom of the rich—not to the extent her mother would've liked—but she was more vulnerable, less of a hypocrite than her parents. Yet she was terrified at the idea of losing her husband. Perhaps her mother was right. It's lust, it's like a fever, it will pass, it will pass, she tried to persuade herself.

So she braved it out, and did her best to turn her feigned indifference into a Zen practice.

———

But it wasn't just lust; Sandro was in love.

For more than a year he had been taking the same early-morning yoga class in a small studio in Monti, not far from the Colosseum. He and three other guys were the only men among a large group of women who ranged from their twenties to seventy-four. He envied how all their bodies easily flexed, and realized how much more rigid the men seemed to be.

One day Emilia appeared as a substitute for Maura, their usual teacher. Maura had had an accident on her bike and Emilia was to take over the class for two months. Her tiny body was strong yet curvy and perfectly proportioned, but her bob of dark hair gained her a sort of boyish allure. The guys exchanged a glance among themselves as though they didn't trust that she would have enough experience, but right away she proved to be a much more adroit instructor. Soon the whole class was panting and huffing in the attempt to replicate the sequences she demonstrated, curling and uncurling, twisting her torso right and left with geometric precision, in seemingly effortless, fluid movements. She encouraged the students to try more challenging poses—"You can do it as long as you keep breathing!"—but at the same time she warned them not to push themselves over the limit—"Don't let your ego take over!"—so that within a couple of weeks everyone felt in their stretches the unexpected progress they'd made. Emilia would walk around the class as the students were holding their asanas and lightly touch their bodies, adjusting them into the right position. A tiny rotation of the hip or a light pressure on a shoulder with the tip of her fingertips was enough to put a body in place so that the prana was magically released and the movements became sweet and painless rather than arduous. She would whisper in the students' ears, words that made them proud of themselves.

"Open your heart—yeah, like this. Aaah, that's it, here you go—that's beautiful!"

Sandro sensed that her touch on him wasn't completely neutral. At first he thought he must be imagining this, that it must be a classic projection, a kind of yogic transference. It was hard to decipher, but he was convinced that something akin to an erotic current flowed from her fingertips to his core. He tried to send back the same message, concentrating on the parts of his body that she touched, and charging them with an equivalent amount of electricity. He also increased his attendance in class from twice a week to three. By then the other men in the class had become respectful of and almost intimidated by her. After class, before getting into the shower, they would linger around the herbal tea corner, where Emilia would sit with her legs crossed on the wooden bench, holding her tiny cup in her palm as the aroma of licorice and mint filled the small space.

Sandro didn't take part in the tea-break ritual. He wanted to have a moment with Emilia without the others watching. One day, feeling bold, he waited for her outside the yoga studio. She was intent on unlocking her bicycle when he approached her.

"Emilia? I have a question for you."

She turned. Her short hair was damp from the shower, and when she turned he saw she'd put on dark-red lipstick. She looked sexy, like a strong and petite French movie star from the sixties.

"Oh, hi. I almost didn't recognize you in your . . . I mean, with clothes on."

She pointed at the *fresco di lana* tailored suit he wore to work.

"Yeah, right. . . . I'm afraid I look different in this. A bit too stiff, is it?"

Emilia laughed, then blushed. She was wearing a faded Indian camisole underneath a vintage jeans jacket and cargo pants. He thought she looked lovely in such a casual, simple outfit. He felt a wave of tenderness.

"No, I didn't mean to . . . Actually, it's very elegant. It suits you," she said.

Sandro's opened arms were a gesture of resignation.

"Slave to a law firm, unfortunately."

"Right," she said, unsure whether she was meant to laugh.

They stared at each other and there was a brief silence, as though they had no idea what should come next. Then Emilia smiled uneasily.

"Yes . . . ? What's the question?"

"Right. . . . It's just a . . . it's a silly question, actually."

"Go on."

"What do you mean exactly when you say, 'Open your heart'? I mean, is it a movement of the chest or a shift in attitude, an inclination?"

Emilia's face lit up.

"It's both. It's a shift, mental and physical. You'll see how everything changes when you become more aware. You really need to open up more, Sandro. To release. I've noticed you are pretty locked up."

Sandro frowned, but it flattered him that she had noticed something about him.

"Am I?"

"Yes."

"Where?"

She placed the tips of her three fingers on his sternum and tapped it lightly.

"Right here."

Sandro inhaled deeply and felt his chest expand. As ever, her touch was magical. He was slightly overwhelmed.

"See?" she said. "You're already opening up."

"Wow. That's impressive."

"We all walk around carrying internal steel barriers, and our bodies mirror that. Opening up the heart not only means coming forward with your chest, but, more profoundly, letting go of your defenses, being open to possibilities and change . . ."

Emilia paused for a second, holding her breath.

"And more open to love, of course," she added.

She still had her fingertips on his sternum, and Sandro felt his heart begin to race. Something inside his rib cage—a surge of air, a tiny creature?—spread its wings and flew out of his lungs, following which, a vigorous erection blossomed.

———

A few days later, after class, Sandro asked Emilia whether she'd like to join him for coffee in a new place that had just opened across the street from the studio. It was the end of the summer, it hadn't rained in months, the city was parched and dusty but that morning the weather had turned. The air felt humid and sticky and it had just begun to drizzle.

They sat near the window while darker clouds clustered in the west; the steam exuding from the heat of the crowd in the café had fogged the windowpanes and it felt cozy and intimate to be sitting inside, tucked in a corner. They tried to jump-start a conversation, but they were both too nervous and overexcited to find a sensible topic. They dropped spoons and cups, and kept giggling, blushing, sweating, unable to concentrate. At one point Emilia casually mentioned the fact that she was married. The revelation she had a husband somehow caught Sandro unprepared. There was an awkward moment of silence, and he perceived a shift in their communication, as though they were entering a new phase, where, in order to proceed in any direction, the exchange of relevant information regarding their status had become imperative. In turn, he mentioned in passing Ottavia and their daughter, Ilaria. He noticed a flash of disappointment dart across Emilia's face.

Thunder rumbled loudly in the distance, then suddenly there was a downpour. Through the fogged glass they could see the trees shaking, lightning flashing behind dark clouds, then rain and hail pelting the cobblestones. People inside the café rejoiced, as if the rain were the gift everyone had been waiting for.

Outside, passersby were waiting under awnings or inside shops for the deluge to taper off, but Sandro quickly paid their check and grabbed Emilia's elbow, and they ran across the street, holding on to each other's arms, exhilarated, getting drenched. Once they reached her bicycle, he didn't let go of her, but pulled her close and kissed her on the lips while rivulets of water ran over their faces and slid inside his collar. Emilia threw her head back and laughed.

"In any case, I'm crazy about you," he announced, somewhat theatrically, before spinning on his heel and running away through the rain.

A week later they had sex for the first time.

———

When the previous yoga instructor had fully recovered from her bike accident, Emilia went back to teaching morning classes at another studio and giving some private lessons. But at that point Sandro no longer needed an excuse to see her, and as a result his interest in yoga dwindled and eventually waned. One month into the affair, he was so smitten by Emilia that he had surprised her by renting a one-bedroom in an anonymous neighborhood on the north side of town. The apartment—it had come with sparse, drab furniture—was to be their safe place, a sort of stage where it was possible to mimic a conjugal life. However, since they were allowed only tiny windows of time away from their usual routines, and they both had to constantly come up with elaborate excuses with Bruno and Ottavia, their encounters were inevitably brief and heartbreaking.

After the first few euphoric rendezvous, their lovemaking became more intense, verging on the dramatic, as though they needed to invest it with the desperation of their imminent separation rather than the solace of being reunited. Such is the fate of adulterers, Sandro would think when he held her tiny frame in his arms. Clandestine love was insatiable, like an eating disorder. There was no joy in it, only desire. No fulfillment, only longing.

Both he and Emilia were suspended in an identical situation. Once their lovemaking was over, they both rushed to their respective phones, checking the time and whether they had missed a message from their respective spouses. They would take a quick shower in the tiny bathroom and rush off into their respective cars, heading in opposite directions toward their respective families.

But now their situation was no longer symmetrical. Emilia could show up late for dinner, forget to pick up groceries. It was easier to make excuses with the girls. They didn't know a thing about trysts and grown-ups' secrets, and if there was no food in the fridge, they would obediently eat cereal.

———

It took a couple of months for Anita and Sofia to perceive what the loss of their father had produced. Once things had quieted down—the shock, the tears and the continuous attention that adults had been showering upon them—they realized that a thin crack had been moving along an invisible path, splitting their world in two. As the fracture deepened, like a running fault line before an earthquake, they felt more and more separated from what was left on the other side of the chasm.

The small garden Bruno had lovingly been caring for since they were tiny was turning into a wild, angry wasteland. When they had first moved into the apartment building in Pigneto—an old working-class neighborhood now undergoing a slow gentrification—the so-called garden at the back of their ground-floor apartment had been just a large patch of dirt, but Bruno prided himself on possessing a green thumb and immediately set to work. He planted all kinds of shrubs, creepers, bulbs and perennials, so that they would continue to flower all year round. Besides the herbaceous plants that would bloom in rotation, he also put in a peach and a plum tree, which he named after each girl, so that a few years later they were already eating Anita-peaches and Sofia-plums. But now, with astonishing speed, the plumbago and lantana bushes had lost their shape and become a tangle of twigs that suffocated the roses; the fruit trees needed pruning, their branches reaching out all the way to their bedroom windows, obscuring the view and punching against the glass, as though begging to be let in. The violent summer heat had sucked the chlorophyll off the hydrangeas' leaves, and now they wilted, bleached by the sun, without sap. The soil had turned back into a dusty crust—one could hardly believe it once had been supple and full of nutrients. Anita and Sofia struggled to recall the deep-green shade the garden had once provided, filled with blooming flowers, sweet scents and butterflies. The familiar image of their father crouching by the flower beds, digging, transplanting, meticulously brushing the artemisia and lavender leaves so they could release their aroma, was already fading away.

Even the apartment had caught a malaise: objects seemed to be slowly losing their will to function. A film of dust—or was it a veil of carelessness?—had infiltrated every recess, so that light bulbs went out but nobody bothered to replace them, the sink clogged, the washer died, but there was no money to replace them.

The lack of money was another change. They had never been rich, but Bruno had always managed to pay for whatever was needed. He had been a sound technician in a sophisticated recording studio, highly sought after by musicians and composers. But he had never had life insurance and had left only a small amount of money in the bank and a mortgage pending on the apartment. All along Bruno had been spending everything he made, thinking he still had time to worry about savings.

Now Emilia needed to find a real job—yoga lessons weren't going to pay the mortgage—but most of the time she was procrastinating, as though some kind of miracle would happen soon and resolve their financial situation. All she did was say, "We can't afford it," whenever the girls asked for something. Whether it was clothes, takeout pizza, a movie.

And then there was Mr. D'Onofrio.

That's how they were supposed to address him, according to Emilia, even though Anita and Sofia had always been on a first-name basis with all of their parents' friends and used surnames only when they talked to teachers, doctors or very old people. But was this Mr. D'Onofrio meant to be a friend? And if so, why couldn't they call him Sandro? How come he had showed up so unexpectedly, and was coming over for dinner as though he were a relative, without anybody else ever being invited? And why, *why*, was he sitting at the head of the dining table, in their father's place?

These were only a few of the questions Anita and Sofia didn't dare pose to their mother. It was an unwritten rule that somehow she had silently established, to which they silently obeyed: they were not to ask, they were to take for granted that this stranger in well-ironed shirts and expensive suede loafers was now a fixture in their home. As though it were natural for her to have a new friend, with whom she seemed to be on quite intimate terms and who had suddenly popped out of nowhere, right after Bruno's disappearance.

But if Sandro D'Onofrio was supposed to be Mamma's new friend, to them he wasn't friendly. If anything, he seemed embarrassed to be sitting with the three of them in front of the elaborate dishes Emilia cooked whenever he showed up. He was polite, but he hardly ever addressed the girls, as though he had no idea how to interact with them, or was afraid they might bite him. Emilia was the only one who seemed completely at ease: cheerful, chatty, somehow ecstatic. She didn't pick up on the tension that ran around the table, or maybe she just pretended not to notice how stilted the conversation was.

"He's married," Anita told Sofia.

They had helped clear the table and had gone back to their room to finish their homework, while Emilia and Sandro were left to chat in the living room. Often the two of them drank Scotch after dinner, a new habit.

"He doesn't have a wedding ring," Sofia pointed out cautiously, sitting cross-legged on her bed.

"Nobody does anymore. That's old-fashioned."

"How can you tell he's married?"

"Why do you think we have to eat so early when he comes around?"

Sofia shrugged. She didn't particularly want to know. Once things were given a name, they became real.

"Because after dinner he goes back to his wife!" Anita sneered. "He probably has to eat twice."

Unlike her little sister, she enjoyed unearthing all that went unsaid.

Sofia made a timid attempt at laughing.

"Really? He's going to gain lots of weight, then."

Anita glared. "She never set the table with two glasses for Papà," she said. "And she was always a shitty cook, before."

Emilia had become a "she." She had turned into someone who had joined the other side of the divide. As the fault line ran quicker and deeper, she was getting farther and farther away from her daughters, along with all the things they had lost.

———

Sandro wasn't sure about the girls.

There was such a rough edge about them: they had bushy eyebrows and dark curls, their knees and legs scabby, always covered in scratches, their nails never clean. On them any piece of clothing looked like some old hand-me-down, washed too many times and never properly ironed. He had a feeling they didn't like to bathe too much, because their hair, unruly and jet-black, smelled of cooked food. He guessed that one day they'd grow into attractive adolescents and then young women, but now they looked too feral and unshaped to be considered pretty.

Emilia had insisted that he come to her place every now and again, to have a quick bite and "get familiar with the girls." He had accepted, only because he didn't have the heart to tell her that he'd rather not.

"I'll tell them the truth, that you're one of my former students and we've become good friends," she'd said.

"Isn't it too soon?"

"We have to start somewhere. I want them to get used to you."

It worried him, this idea of familiarization. Did it mean that somewhere along the line they too were going to be a family? It seemed so farfetched and maybe, deep down, not what he wanted. He still wanted Emilia, but he could do without all the baggage that came with her. Not to mention those painful flashes of Ottavia and his daughter that tore like unwanted reminders through his reveries.

———

Where to start with Anita and Sofia? He would bring ice cream or pastries from a French patisserie when he came to dinner, but the girls never thanked him. He asked them about school, whether they liked it and if they had good grades, but they mumbled something incomprehensible, avoiding his eyes. He bought a couple of books his daughter had loved (Ilaria was an avid reader), and gave them to Anita. She didn't look interested; she didn't ever open them and left them on the kitchen counter when she went back to her room. He tried to engage Sofia by asking what kind of music she liked, but the girl looked at her older sister, as if asking permission to answer his questions. Anita made a face and shrugged. Sofia turned to him and said she didn't really listen to music much. Even the cat sprang from the couch and ran off each time he entered the living room.

He didn't like to come to the part of the city where they lived; it was on the opposite side from where he lived, and very different. He seemed to remember that Pasolini had set one of his movies in Pigneto (he vaguely remembered stark black-and-white scenes in a squalid neighborhood), but he had never had a reason to drive through it and frankly he found it depressing. But more than that, it surprised him how neglected and messy Emilia's home was, like a student's place, how cheap the furniture, assembled without logic or taste. He'd much prefer to see her in their rented apartment at the other end of town, which was neutral and spotless (he paid a housecleaner to come once a week). When Emilia mentioned that keeping the apartment was an expense he and they could now do without, he told her there were boundaries that had to be respected, and that he'd never agree to have sex in what used to be Emilia's marital bed. They needed to have a space that was theirs and theirs only, with no trace of their pasts. She apologized and agreed.

So far the meals with the girls had been painful. Yet Emilia kept pretending not to notice. Her denial was beginning to disturb him.

They hadn't finished eating yet when Anita stood up.

"You should ask permission to leave the table," Sandro snapped.

He didn't even know where that had come from, and the minute he said it, he knew it had been a mistake. It was childish, but he felt it was time to teach her a lesson. Anita scowled. She stood still.

"Why?" she said, her eyes dark and mean.

"Because that's what kids have to do."

He pointed to the chair.

"Sit down. We're not finished yet."

There was a brief silence. Anita turned toward her mother, waiting for her to come to her aid. But Emilia kept her eyes on the plate, pretending nothing was required of her. Anita turned back to him, defiantly.

"You can't tell me what to do. You're not my father."

"I know I'm not. Still, you should ask your mother for permission."

Emilia pressed a hand on Anita's shoulder, trying to push her back down into the chair. Anita shook her off.

"Don't touch me!"

Then she turned to Sandro and repeated, shouting in his face, "You're not my father!"

Sofia looked frightened, as if, by mentioning the word *father,* Anita had exposed the truth everyone around them had tried to conceal: how they had become helpless, at the mercy of any stranger.

Anita caught her by the arm and yanked her off the chair.

"Come on, let's go."

"Anita! Stop it!" Emilia grabbed her by the T-shirt. "Come back immediately!"

But Anita pulled away abruptly. There was a tear, the shirt ripped.

"I hate you! I hate you both!" she yelled and disappeared, dragging Sofia behind her.

Emilia put her elbows on the table and rested her face behind her hands for a couple of seconds. Then she shook her head ruefully.

"I'm so sorry. They're out of control. I sometimes just don't know what to do with them anymore," she said, as if her own children had become strangers who temporarily occupied a space she wished she didn't have to share.

As he drove across town to get home that night, Sandro couldn't shake off the feeling that he was responsible for Emilia's estrangement from her daughters. And it worried him how indifferent she seemed, how unconcerned about their needs. He and Emilia had gone too far, in a direction that was leading nowhere—now he could see how delusional they both had been, how they hadn't seriously considered the consequences, ignoring how many people were going to be hurt and scarred. They had been too careless, he thought, as he parked the car along the sidewalk of his leafy street in Parioli. How quiet and civilized his neighborhood felt at that time of night. According to Emilia, Bruno had never suspected anything, and now that he was dead, Sandro was the only one left dealing with the guilt, the shame and the lies. It was unfair, he caught himself thinking as he got out of the car, but part of him actually resented feeling that way.

It was nearly ten when he walked into his apartment. The lights were dimmed low and the living room was awash in a warm orange glow. He found Ottavia curled up on the sofa, reading a magazine, wrapped in a light caftan they had bought in Morocco a few years before. She lifted her eyes from the page.

"Hi, darling, have you had something to eat yet? There's food for you in the fridge."

"I'm fine, thank you—I grabbed sushi with a client. How was your day?"

"Great. We almost finished installing the show. I'm exhausted, but it's going to look amazing. You should pop in when you have a moment."

"I will. Maybe tomorrow at lunchtime?"

"Yes. I'd like to hear what you think before we're done."

"Sure. Where is Ilaria?"

"In her room, studying. Tomorrow she has that big math test."

He leaned over her and kissed her lightly on the head. Her skin had a fresh, lemony smell.

Ilaria was sitting at her desk, her hair tied in a loose bun. His studious, earnest daughter. Sandro sat on her bed, across from her. There was a half-opened book, facedown, on the bedspread. He peeked at the title: *Pride and Prejudice*.

"Ciao, Papà."

Ilaria brushed a strand of hair away from her forehead and placed it behind her ear. She had lost weight lately, her elbows and knees bony, her legs like sticks. Too much time indoors, too much homework, Sandro thought. He hardly ever came into her room, which was tidy and strangely unadorned for that of a twelve-year-old. No posters or photos on the wall, only a couple of botanical prints that Ottavia had bought when they had first moved in, no nail polish, perfumes or beauty products on the shelf, no clothes or socks strewn on the floor. He made a mental note to spend more time with her, take her to the opera, to museums and movies. Quality time with his daughter was essential; soon she'd turn into a teenager and he and Ottavia would probably lose sight of her.

"What's wrong?" Ilaria said. "You look sad."

Sandro immediately stood up.

"Sad? No, why? I'm not sad. I'm happy to be home, happy to see you."

Ilaria stared at him for a couple of seconds as though she didn't know him, as if he too had turned into a stranger who had agreed to live temporarily with her and Ottavia in the same house. Sandro felt alone for the first time since he had started hiding from his child and wife. We don't have much time before it's too late, he thought, and he wasn't sure whether he meant too late as in ending his affair, or too late as in losing his family.

———

The therapist was a gentle woman in her sixties with a tangle of curly gray hair, chunky amber beads around her neck. Her top-floor studio behind Piazza Cavour was filled with orchids, all of them vigorously in bloom and clearly well cared for. A light breeze from the open window kept curling the edges of a stack of papers pressed under a crystal weight.

"Anorexia?" Ottavia repeated, stupefied. As if she didn't know already. All the signs were there, had been for at least three months. The weight loss, the excuses Ilaria found each time she was offered any food.

The woman nodded.

"I think it will be necessary for you and your husband to come in with Ilaria."

"You mean, like . . . family therapy?"

"Yes. Certain issues may be resolved faster if we are all together in one room. It's the only way to explore and work through the overall ability of the family to function. Ilaria's body is clearly reacting to something and she's using her body to express the anger and the pain she feels."

Ottavia stared at her, baffled.

"Yes, yes, of course, you're right. I just don't know if my husband is . . ."

She looked around the room, at all those flowers, at the

stains of moist color that suddenly seemed too violent in the bright light.

"I mean, whether he will agree to . . . He doesn't believe in therapy; he's the type of man who . . ."

She paused.

"I haven't even told him I took Ilaria to see you."

"Why not?"

Ottavia felt herself blush.

"I thought maybe I was overreacting. . . . I didn't realize it was so serious. I thought maybe Ilaria was just stressed because of school. Maybe a little depressed, or—"

The therapist interrupted her.

"She *is* depressed. It's obviously part of a much larger problem."

She brushed the amber beads with her fingertips, and kept one rolling between her thumb and second finger. Ottavia stared at the necklace and wondered where it came from. Ethiopia? Tibet? Was this woman an adventurous traveler? She didn't look like one.

"I'm sure your husband will agree to come in once he understands the situation. You were not overreacting. Anorexia is a very serious disorder, especially at such a young age. In the long run it can be life-threatening."

Ottavia shifted uncomfortably on the chair.

"Yes. He will, certainly. I mean, he's just very busy at work. . . . He's a senior partner in a big international law firm, so we'll have to schedule around his—"

The therapist put on reading glasses with bright-red plastic frames.

"Oh, I'm sure he'll find forty-five minutes for Ilaria," she said, tapping a pen on a small calendar she had in front of her. "I'd first like to see just the two of you without her. Let's see . . . how about Tuesday at ten past three?"

———

So there they were, both sitting across from the woman with amber beads, like two criminals in an interrogation room filled with orchids. Sandro had agreed to come in without putting up any resistance and Ottavia had a feeling they were both ready to confess; all they needed was the right question.

"Is there anything you think might have sparked Ilaria's condition?"

They exchanged a quick glance.

"Not that we know of," Ottavia said, then turned to her husband. "Right?"

"Any problems at home? Anything I need to know?" the therapist prodded them.

Ottavia was the first to collapse. She blurted it out in a flood of tears while the therapist kept handing her tissues. Sandro admitted everything. He felt a knot in his throat a couple of times, but somehow unburdening in front of this woman he'd never seen before was easier than he'd imagined. She wasn't judgmental, her questions were neutral, she wasn't trying to make him feel guilty. She suggested they also go see someone to sort out their situation as a couple, and referred them to a colleague. Ottavia stopped crying at last. She quieted down and became attentive. Suddenly Sandro felt her hand searching for his. He took it. In the space of forty-five minutes, what had seemed to him impossible to do was done. He was holding his wife's hand, they were both ready to face whatever they had to for the sake of their daughter. They were a family and they were going to be a team. And that was that.

———

It was the end of September and there was a new crispness in the air. Short gusts of wind shook the trees in the garden.

D'Onofrio had vanished from their lives and, with his exit, Emilia had shrunken and paled. There had been crying behind doors, whispering on the phone, some pleading. Then silence. She became listless, irritable, at times abrupt. She made herself unavailable, uninterested in Anita and Sofia, in what was going on at school or with their friends. Often she forgot to change their bedsheets, run the washing machine. She canceled her morning classes at the yoga studio, listened to a lot of baleful music, slept during the day at odd hours, drank what was left of the bottle of Scotch.

The girls didn't talk, didn't comment on that sadness and its cause. By then they had learned to communicate with each other the way cats do, as though they had developed a sixth sense or a secret language. They could read the subtle mutations of Emilia's grief based on the flow of air throughout the rooms, the sound of her breath, her movements, her smell. And, like cats, they moved around the apartment softly, their footfalls padded, so as not to intrude on her stillness.

The girls waited, patiently, for this mourning to subside, the mourning that their mother should've felt for Bruno but hadn't. Despite the injustice of it, her despair was more bearable than the euphoria, the rapture, the silly laughter at the table, the blindness. They waited because even though she wasn't present, now at least she was back—limp and sometimes slightly drunk, captive to the couch or the bedroom—and they knew she wasn't going to leave them.

Anita eagerly took over the shopping. She scanned the supermarket aisles, looking for discounts and offers. She made grilled-cheese sandwiches for lunch and instant soups and toast for dinner, every single day. She wanted Emilia to ingest something warm and soothing, hoping it could reawaken her. It was like playing dolls again, having to feed her mother as if she were her daughter.

Then, one night, Emilia was slouched on the couch watching television when Anita sat next to her holding her cup of soup. Emilia started combing Anita's hair absentmindedly with the tips of her fingers.

"Your hair has grown so much, sweetie," Emilia said, as if she'd just realized how much time had passed. "Go get a hair band in the bathroom—I'll braid it for you."

Anita ran, and came back eager for Emilia to start.

"Come here, closer. Sit on my lap."

Anita sat still, holding her breath, feeling her mother's fingers move nimbly through her hair, tightening the braid. Sofia appeared, and, as she saw the two of them so close, climbed up on the couch like a kitten.

"Can you braid my hair too?" she asked apprehensively.

"Of course. Just wait till I finish with Ninni."

Emilia had used Anita's old nickname—it had been a long time since she had called her that.

"Can we watch a film together?" Anita immediately asked. She didn't want to move away from that closeness.

Emilia handed her the remote. "Yes. Pick what you like."

The girls curled up next to her. Emilia took them under her arms, one on each side, their arms and legs in a tangle.

They fell asleep halfway through the film, their warm, soupy breaths mingled into one in a steady rhythm.

———

They came through the door followed by a whiff of December cold. A tall, handsome woman, her teenage daughter and two older people, the grandparents, most probably. Good-looking, elegant, clearly a family, they were laughing, moving around at ease, like people used to having the world at their feet.

Anita watched them as the waiters greeted the group with familiarity, took their coats, led them to a corner table at the end of the room. It was the kind of old-fashioned restaurant near Piazza di Spagna now getting harder to find in the city, with etchings of ancient Rome on the walls, dark wooden paneling, white tablecloths and elderly waiters way past their retirement age. A couple of minutes later the door opened again with a slight creaking sound and Sandro walked in, car keys in hand, a thick scarf wrapped around his neck. Anita recognized him at once as he, without seeing them, hurried past the table where she was sitting with Emilia and Sofia, leaving a trail of his familiar scent. English Fern cologne. He reached the corner table, joined the family chatter, shook the hand of the headwaiter, who greeted him by name, kissed his daughter. Suddenly Emilia looked up from the dessert menu and her face turned to stone.

"Oh, fuck," she said.

"What?" Sofia asked, alarmed.

"Fuck, fuck, fuck."

Emilia's hands tormented the napkin, then she took a deep breath as if she couldn't fill her lungs with enough air.

"I think we should go," she said.

"No, Mamma. Why?" Anita asked.

Emilia glared at her.

"Because."

"I don't want to leave yet. We still have to have dessert."

It was Anita's birthday. It had been Emilia's idea to take them to lunch in a nice restaurant. The one Anita had picked was rather expensive, but Emilia agreed that turning thirteen was a big deal and deserved a proper celebration. Anita had asked permission to book the table herself; making the reservation under her own name had made her feel very grown up.

"You don't understand. I don't feel well," Emilia said firmly.

Her face had become strangely solid, as if she had a plastic film tightly wrapped over her skin.

Anita ignored her and shot a glance at the table at the end of the room. Sandro was sitting with his back to them, so she couldn't see his face. But she could see his daughter, whom she realized was about her own age. How slim, pretty, how protected and safe she looked in her light-blue turtleneck, her designer jeans and lace-up boots. Obviously, Anita thought, she would've been completely shielded from what she and Sofia had been exposed to—all the lies, the deceit. Having Sandro sit at their table for months on end, like a family member? Oh, please. What a joke.

Sandro must've said something funny because the girl was laughing now; even the mother seemed amused and was whispering something in the girl's ear, which made her laugh even more. Look at them. Unscathed.

"Why don't you go and say hi to him?" Anita turned toward Emilia defiantly.

"Stop it."

"No, really. Why can't you go and say hi? What are you afraid of? He's a friend of yours, no?"

Sofia, once again, looked terrified. She was pleading with her eyes for her sister to stop.

"Sofia, please ask for the check," Emilia said and began to rummage in her faded canvas handbag, keeping her head down.

Anita felt a surge of anger, seeing her mother turn into a victim once again. Why did they have to run away, like people proven wrong, who had something to hide? Why were they always at the mercy of someone else?

"It's my birthday. I want dessert. I'm not leaving," Anita repeated.

Emilia snarled, "You do whatever the fuck you want. I'm leaving now."

Emilia grabbed the leather jacket hanging on the back of the chair and began to heave like someone gasping for her last breath. Then she bent over, retching, and threw up on the table. The restaurant went quiet and people turned their heads. Emilia stood up, kicked back the chair that crashed on the floor and ran outside. At that instant Sandro looked over his shoulder, and Anita caught his eyes, the surprise and terror in them, like someone seeing a train coming at him too fast.

———

With her eyes closed, lips slightly parted, Emilia lay on the sidewalk outside the restaurant next to a fancy flower shop. An unsightly scene for such a pristine neighborhood. The street was quiet, tucked away in a pedestrian area where only taxis were allowed. A couple of passersby had stopped and were leaning over her. Someone had covered her with the leather jacket she had grabbed on the way out but hadn't had time to put on. A bald man with glasses was on his knees, patting her face lightly. Anita and Sofia shot out of the restaurant.

"What happened?" Anita screamed. "What's wrong with her?"

"Is this your mother?" the man asked.

Anita nodded, unable to speak.

"She passed out, but she'll be all right," the man said.

A young woman in a thick synthetic fur came running from the café across the street, holding a paper cup. She handed it to the kneeling man, who, in the space of thirty seconds, seemed to have become the one in charge of their mother's life. He splashed a few drops on Emilia's face, then lifted her head, trying to make her take a sip. Her skin was white, almost translucent, and had softened like Play-Doh.

"Does your mom have low blood pressure? Do you know?" the man asked Anita. "Is she on any medications?"

Anita shook her head, terrified. She had no idea.

"Is she allergic to something? Diabetic?"

"No, no."

More people stopped, asked questions, whispered.

Sofia burst out crying. "Is she going to die?"

The woman who had brought the paper cup stroked her hair. Anita felt a sharp, cold pain like teeth gnawing at her stomach.

"No, sweetheart. She'll be fine, she just needs a little sugar . . ." the woman said, but exchanged a nervous glance with the man in charge. The woman pulled out her phone and leaned close to him.

"Should we call an ambulance?"

The man made a gesture as if to prevent the woman from saying more, as if she was overreacting.

"Let's wait. I don't think it's necessary."

He turned to the girls.

"Where is your father?" he asked with a hint of impatience. "Is he with you?"

Anita nodded slowly, as if in a trance.

"Please go get him. Now."

Anita, without saying a word, turned around and ran back inside. She bumped shoulders with a waiter who was gathering the dirty linens from their table in a bundle. Anita ran to the end of the room, grabbed Sandro by the sleeve. Her heart was beating in her chest so fast she thought it was going to crack any minute. Out of the corner of her eye she saw Sofia, still sobbing, who had followed behind her.

"Please come outside and help her. She's dying!"

Just pronouncing the word made Anita's knees nearly give in, her vision blur. How could this happen so quickly? Was the world coming to an end? She saw the handsome blond woman's face crumble in slow motion—the wife, who else?—but she held her gaze steadily on Sandro and kept tugging at him, her five fingers clutched around his wrist.

"Get up! We need to call an ambulance—I told you she's dying!"

As if he were her property, she yanked him from the table. Her peripheral vision caught the stupefied expression of the grandparents and Ottavia shaking her head in despair and disbelief. As Sandro stood up she heard the girl's voice, childish and yet strangely strident.

"Papi, where are you going. . . . Papi, why?"

Sandro didn't put forth any resistance; he followed the girls across the room and through the creaking doors with the restaurant's name etched in gold in an old-fashioned font.

He couldn't have done otherwise: this had to be the last act, the closing one.

————

When they reached the small crowd gathered on the sidewalk, Emilia was already sitting up. Her gaze was unfocused, otherworldly, her face drained of color. The bald man was still kneeling next to her, helping her into her leather jacket. As soon as Sandro appeared, followed by the girls, everyone made space for him to come through. The bald man stood up, shook Sandro's hand.

"I'm a doctor—your wife just fainted. Her pulse is stable now; it could be just a hypoglycemic episode. She looks okay now but I'd take her to the emergency room, just to be safe."

Sandro nodded slightly, not contradicting him. He and Emilia exchanged a glance. She made a gesture with her hand that shrugged off the man's assumption. People stared, confused, at this brief interaction and at the awkward distance that remained between them. Sofia and Anita were standing behind Sandro, holding hands.

"Should we call an ambulance?" Sandro asked.

Emilia stretched her arm toward the doctor, who helped her stand up.

"No, we'll take a taxi. It's fine. I'm okay, really."

She stood up. She looked beautiful and tragic, a delicate, tiny thing. The short bob of dark hair was stuck to her damp skin and the film of sweat made it glow like a pearl. The dress she was wearing was stained and crumpled. She smelled like vomit.

Sandro stood, uncertain, with too many eyes fixed on him. He looked lost.

"Are you sure? I can drive you home if—"

Emilia stopped him with her open palm.

"No. Anita will call a cab."

She handed her bag to her daughter.

"You do that, my love."

Right at that moment they saw a taxi come their way. Anita ran to the curb and hailed it.

"It was just a spell, nothing to worry about. Thank for your kindness," Emilia said to the doctor, ignoring Sandro.

Sofia and Anita grabbed her hands from each side and led her toward the taxi. Before getting in, Emilia turned toward Sandro, who was still standing on the sidewalk.

"Could you take care of the check? I forgot to pay the bill."

As the car drove off Anita turned around and gave a last look at Sandro through the rear window. He was surrounded by the few onlookers who had come to Emilia's rescue, looking lost, like an actor who has forgotten his lines and has no clue as to what to do next.

———

In the back of the taxi Anita and Sofia huddled against Emilia. Anita pressed her body as close as possible to her mother's and sniffed her.

"You stink," she said and repressed a giggle.

Emilia looked out of the window.

"I know. I'm disgusting."

Sofia whispered into the curve of her mother's neck, "Can we all take a bath when we get home?"

Emilia nodded and ran her hand through Sofia's hair.

"Today it's Anita's birthday and you both get to do everything you want," she said. "But only for twenty-four hours, remember. Then I'm the boss again."

She leaned back on the headrest and closed her eyes. Her breathing got deeper almost instantly. Astonishingly, she had fallen asleep. Anita stared at the miracle of her mother's chest rising and falling, at the faint beat of her pulse visible through the inside of her wrist. As if moved by a mysterious instinct, Anita reached for the soft spot beneath Emilia's neck, the small, hollow dent right between her collarbones. She placed two fingertips on it, feeling the warmth of the veins pumping blood into her mother's heart, and left them there, as if conjuring a powerful spell. A magical trick that, she believed, would disperse everyone's unhappiness and keep them safe forever and ever, till the end of time.

THE GIRL

It was the summer of '88.

As he came around the bend of the road, he saw the girl. She was crouching under the shade of a large fig tree. At first, all he could make out was the white of her floppy trousers, the colorful Indian shirt, the leather sandals. She gave a last bite to a plump fruit she must've picked from the tree, threw half of it behind her and waved her open palm forcefully, as if she owned the road and were ordering him to stop the car. He did, and as he turned off the engine the only sound he heard in the blazing afternoon was the hysterical song of the cicadas screeching at their highest pitch.

The girl bent over, peeked inside the battered station wagon, and glanced at the bright red interior. He caught a flash of her green eyes, her chestnut hair tied in a wispy braid. She looked to be in her early twenties. An acrid smell emanated from her skin, like hay and dust. Once she determined that he was alone, or maybe that the car was to her liking, she placed a hand on the door.

"I'm going just a few kilometers up the road."

"Get in," he said.

She pulled a canvas bag from behind a bush and threw it next to the large wooden crates that took most of the space in the back. She sat in the passenger seat and made another gesture with her hand, pointing at the road ahead of them. She didn't smile or thank him.

"It's very hot today," he said, but she didn't answer, just nodded and pulled up the bottom of her shirt to wipe off the sweat from her forehead, revealing a strip of white flesh beneath her belly button. There was a protracted silence as he drove on the narrow road that zigzagged through the olive trees and the prickly pears protected by low stone walls. The girl kept looking out from her side, as if she were searching for something. She stretched her arm outside the window and moved her hand, clutching and opening her fist, moving her fingers against the hot air as if she wanted to grab it. He glanced at the nape of her neck, taking in once again the smell of her unwashed hair. He noticed the rings, the cheap jewelry on her wrists.

"Do you live around here?" he asked.

"No. Not anymore. My parents do."

"Are you visiting them?"

The girl nodded.

"Just for a couple of days. My sister is getting married."

"And where do you live now?"

"Here and there. I was in Greece for a few months. I took the ferry back and hitched all the way up here."

"Where are you going back to? After you visit your parents, I mean."

She looked at him warily. Her voice hardened.

"I'm meeting some friends in Naples next week. Maybe we'll go to France. We know some people we can stay with. They live on a farm."

"You don't have a job? I mean, how do you make your money?"

The girl shrugged.

"We work where we can. In Greece we sold these bracelets on the street." She pulled up her wrist to show him. "In France we may work in the vineyards. Pick fruit. I don't know—we'll see."

He registered the "we." It was supposed to let him know she wasn't alone. He didn't want to alarm her, so he drove on, quiet again. She pointed at a turnoff.

"Here. You can leave me here, by that red pole."

"Here? I can drive you all the way to your parents' place."

"It's fine. It's only a ten-minute walk."

"It's blistering hot. Let me take you," he said.

She stared at him—was she gauging whether she could trust him? She had seemed relaxed up until then. He tried not to look at her tiny breasts pushing through the cotton of her shirt. His heart skipped a beat. He mustn't lose her so soon.

"I'm not in a hurry," he said.

The girl had already grabbed her bag from the back seat. She let it go.

"Okay. Follow that road."

He took the turn by the red pole and drove slowly on the narrow drive, winding through the unkempt fields.

"The house is a short way up the hill." She pointed ahead.

A couple of abandoned toolsheds appeared through a large olive grove. He turned to her.

"How are you planning to go to France? Will you hitchhike again?"

"I don't know yet. Why?"

"I could give you a ride if you need one. I'll be heading north in a couple of days."

She didn't answer, just raised her shoulders as if she weren't interested. They had come to a half-broken gate. He could see a house behind a large walnut tree.

He insisted.

"A train to France? It'll cost you money."

"You can stop here."

The girl grabbed her bag from the back seat and reached for the door handle.

"It depends. Maybe we'll take the train, maybe we'll get a ride. I don't know."

She slid out before he could say anything. He watched her open the gate and walk toward the house. After a few steps she turned around, gave him a last look and raised a hand, impatiently, to wave him off.

———

As she walked away, she listened to the rusty station wagon reverse behind her and turn around. At last he had given up. Anybody could smell his loneliness. He looked old, although he was probably only in his early forties, but the way he was dressed in that oppressive heat—tight fuchsia shirt, fake crocodile shoes, hair dyed with what seemed like matte shoe polish—made him look ancient. Or maybe just ridiculous. He had spoken with a foreign accent, German or Russian— she couldn't tell. On the way up she had caught him glancing at her nipples showing through the shirt—but she had hitch-hiked several hundred kilometers and was used to men doing that.

The house looked different. The paint was peeling off the walls and the garden seemed overgrown. Everything had aged: the dogs, the rusty tractor under the shed, her parents, who came out to greet her, uneasily, as usual. They weren't sure they should kiss her.

The girl hadn't seen them in two years, but she imme-diately recognized her father's acid breath, the smell of car grease on his skin. Her mother's furrow between the eyebrows had dug in deeper and her mouth had become a thin line. Something had always been eating her from the inside— probably unhappiness gnawing at her core—and now it had turned her into a dry, brittle husk.

The three of them ate in silence the same midday meal they were used to having every day since she could remem-ber: tomatoes with dried oregano and onions, bread, a slice of fresh ricotta, some leftover beans. Even the oilcloth that cov-ered the table—the yellow one with the cherries—was the same one they had been using since she was a child. The girl recognized nearly every stain like a map she knew by heart. Some things changed so fast and others never did.

Her father broke the silence.

"So, how was it, over there?"

"Where?"

"At the farm."

"It was okay."

The father made a disparaging sound and scowled.

"What?" the girl asked. "What's that supposed to mean?"

The father shook his head and kept chewing his food with his mouth open. The mother glanced at her, signaling she shouldn't say more.

"They told us you left before it was time. They phoned here, asking if we knew where you had gone," the mother said. "But we didn't know where to find you."

"I left because I was done with what I had to do. I was okay—I didn't need to stay any longer."

She stared at them defiantly.

"I'm fine now. There was no point in staying on."

The father snorted, then pushed the plate away.

"Well, let's hope you stay that way."

The farm, way up north, was actually a rehab center, but her parents had always refused to call it that. It was run by a young priest, and the previous year she had been assigned to work in the stable. "Hippotherapy" it was called, from the Greek word for *horse,* someone told her, and it was part of the program. Every morning, along with a few other kids, she groomed the horses. She scrubbed their sides with a brush, feeling their muscles, combed their manes and tails, then washed their nostrils and mouths with a damp sponge. She kissed them on the neck and above their noses and pressed her forehead against theirs. She never got to ride them because they were too old, and most of them were injured, but she had dreams at night that she was riding Bandito, her favorite one, through a thick forest, feeling his back between her legs.

She worked at the stable full-time, and taking care of the horses helped her. She stayed focused and away from drugs.

But it wasn't just that—the horses had become like real people to her. Each morning, when she saw them, she felt her heart racing like mad.

The few times she spoke on the phone with her parents, they made no inquiries about her health and they never came to visit. It was too far, they said, and besides they couldn't leave their own animals alone. To the neighbors they said she had found a job in a barn, up in the north, near Lucca, where she was making good money.

———

Her older sister, Teresa, was out, the mother said with an air of importance; she was with the seamstress up in the next village. There were last-minute alterations to be made to the wedding dress. The father scoffed, saying the dress had been expensive, that it was unreasonable to spend that much money on something you wear only once, all the while the mother kept her eyes on the plate and said nothing. But surely she was the one who had insisted on buying it. The girl knew what it would mean for her mother to have her older daughter show up in church in a tulle dress for everyone to see.

The minute she pulled out the bag of tobacco, her father snickered.

"Now you smoke drugs in my house?"

Her voice tightened.

"Don't be ridiculous—it's tobacco!"

He said nothing but he let out an angry huff of breath.

"Let's not start," she lashed out at him. "I can leave now if you prefer—it makes no difference to me."

"Please, leave her alone," the mother whispered to her husband. She had probably foreseen that they would clash—it was inevitable—and beforehand she must have pleaded with him to keep calm. It was just going to be a few days. No reason to pick a fight.

Later her mother came into her room—the room she had shared with her sister and which had now become her sister's private kingdom.

"Did you buy a dress for the ceremony?" her mother asked. The crease on her forehead looked so deep, it was like a cut.

The girl pulled out something from her sack. It was a pink macramé dress. In view of the wedding, she had done some shoplifting.

The mother sighed.

"Not this one. It's see-through. And it's too short."

"I like it. It's going to be fine."

The mother sat on the bed.

"I was hoping . . . for once . . ."

"What?"

The woman raised her shoulders and looked down at her feet.

"That for once you would try to be respectful. That you would make an effort, just this once. But no. It has to be your way. Always."

"I've made an *effort*. I'm *here*, I've come all the way from Greece just to see you. I've traveled for days to make it on time. This is my effort. It's you who doesn't see it."

She crumpled the dress and threw it angrily across the room.

It was no use. She couldn't find a way to be with them, not even now that she was clean.

Soon the house went silent, both her parents having retired to their bedroom for a siesta, as they always did to get a break from the heat. The girl tried to doze off in her old bed, but a mix of anger and restlessness kept her awake. She got up and opened the closet, searching for something familiar, anything that might make the time she had spent in that house real again. Behind the stacks of her sister's neatly folded clothes, she found a couple of dresses she used to wear when she was around fifteen, when she still longed to look like everyone else. Rummaging in the drawers of the cupboard, she found an envelope containing a few prints of the same photo. It showed her and her sister under the walnut tree on the day of their first communion. Despite the three years' difference, the sisters took communion on the same day so that their parents wouldn't have to pay for two receptions. There they were: two unhappy little girls holding hands, looking more like orphans, or penitent nuns, wrapped in the unshapely white tunics their mother had stitched over the course of one afternoon. She remembered the rest of the girls from the village who were taking the communion on that same day— how proudly they had followed their parents into the church, covered in lace, looking like angels or miniature brides. Staring at the photo, she could almost feel the coarseness of the cheap material on her skin again, the burning disappointment. No money had ever been worth spending on them. At least her sister was getting her reward at last. She was about to walk again through that same church, like the princess she had always wanted to be.

It was only going to be forty-eight hours, she thought. She could do it.

Her sister came back from the seamstress around five with the latest news on the alterations of the dress. They hugged, briefly, wary of each other.

"Oh my God, it's been so long. You've been away forever," Teresa said, then quickly moved away. She glanced at her image in the small mirror hanging on a wall, and tied her hair in a bun with an elastic band.

"Did you miss me?" the girl asked, with a hint of sarcasm.

Teresa looked at her, not sure how to respond.

"Of course I did," she said nonchalantly. "But you were crazy to disappear like that. Mamma at one point thought you might be dead."

The girl looked away, annoyed.

"I was in Greece. It was expensive to call."

Teresa raised an eyebrow.

"Thank God you finally decided to spend the money— otherwise you would've missed my wedding. We had no idea how to reach you."

There was a short silence. Then the sister took the girl's braid in her hand and studied it.

"I like your hair like this. Did you highlight it?"

"No, it's bleached by the sun."

Teresa stepped back and studied her.

"You lost weight," she said. "I'm so fat, I need to shed at least five kilos." She grabbed one of her thighs and pinched it. "Look at this. I hate it."

"You look fine. I promise you," the girl said, even though it was true that her sister had gained too much weight and her complexion looked pasty and uneven.

"So, who is this Vito?"

"You've never met him. He's from farther south, near the cape, but he left and went to work in a hotel in the mountains near Bolzano for five years. He came back last summer, and now he's opened a hardware store near us, in Corigliano. That's how we met. He moved back because he said he missed the sun."

Teresa turned her back again and started rummaging in the cupboard.

"He's good-looking," she added.

For a moment the girl regretted having arrived only a day before the wedding. She wished the two of them could have more time, get reacquainted and exchange secrets like they used to, but her sister seemed too busy to pay attention to her anyway. She was rummaging through the room, opening drawers, looking for things, while the girl stood, unsure as to what to do. Then Teresa looked at her, almost surprised to find her still in the same spot.

"So," she asked, "are you okay now?"

"You want to know if I'm still using?"

"Well, yes."

"I'm clean."

"Good."

The fact of this was all Teresa seemed to need to know, as though it were a minor detail, without narratives and complexities attached. But the girl sensed that her sister might be afraid of learning any of the details. Teresa, she realized, was actually ashamed of her. There was nothing much happening in the village; people always talked and gossiped, and her friends surely knew about the drugs, the rehab. Even her future husband had probably heard. Time to change the subject, she thought.

"And what about you?" the girl blurted out with a trace of hostility. "Are you in love with Vito?"

Teresa snorted, irritated.

"Of course. Would I marry him otherwise?" Then she looked at her small watch. "Sorry, I've got to go check on something."

She turned around, called their mother, who was hanging the laundry outside, and left the girl standing there as she went outside in the backyard.

Teresa spent the rest of the day around the house in a pink polyester slip, checking that everything was under control—the food for the reception, the flowers, the veil, her shoes—while a girlfriend painted her nails, hands and feet, another washed her long dark hair in the sink. For once everyone had to listen to her requests; even her father was given small tasks, like running to the supermarket in town to buy an extra pair of sheer stockings and body lotion. For one day she was allowed to be tearful, fragile and euphoric, and she enjoyed every small crisis that arose in what seemed a sad imitation of a Hollywood actress getting ready for her red-carpet night.

———

The ceremony in church and the big lunch under the walnut tree went fast. By six o' clock everything was over. All that was left in the garden were dirty plates, crumpled napkins, half-empty bottles. Even Teresa's dress—which the girl had to admit was quite spectacular—by the end of the meal had wilted and lost its shimmer. The hem was soiled with the dirt it had picked up as the bride trailed back and forth among the guests. Her makeup had started to melt, her curls to slacken.

The girl felt a certain pity for what was in store for her older sister: the scrawny husband, with those mean eyes and the stupid Laurel and Hardy tattoo, who would eventually become estranged and probably abusive. The sex that in the years to come she would have to surrender to, even when she no longer wanted it. The pregnancies, the babies crying all night, their smelly diapers and baby food becoming her full-time job. The boredom, the feeling of being trapped, without the audacity to break away from a failed marriage. Time would go by and one day, before she was even old, the furrow would show up on her forehead as well.

———

He stopped the station wagon outside the gate and walked in. The yard was silent; the old dogs were asleep in the sun and they didn't get up when he passed them by. He stepped in the kitchen through the half-opened door and breathed the garlicky smell of cooked food. In the semidarkness he saw the woman rinsing something in the sink. An older man was sitting at the table in the back of the kitchen.

"Good morning," he said politely. "I'm here to see your daughter."

The woman wiped her hands on her apron and came closer. Stout, with a bad haircut and tight lips, but he recognized the green eyes. She frowned.

"Which daughter?"

He realized he didn't even know her name.

"The one who arrived the other day. For the wedding."

The husband stood up. He too was weathered, coarse. Farmer's hands, dry skin. Still chewing something. He seemed alarmed and intimidated at the same time.

"Who are you?"

"Hello, my name is Andor Antal."

He offered his hand and put on a smile. He didn't want to scare them.

"What do you want?" The man didn't take his hand.

"It's about a job. I met your daughter the other day. I'm interested in hiring her."

The man and the woman stared at each other.

"What kind of a job?" asked the father.

Andor paused. Then he smiled again, as politely as he could.

"Is it possible to speak to her for a minute? I'm in a bit of a hurry."

That seemed to do it. The woman went into the next room, while Andor stood there, under the silent gaze of the father.

The girl appeared on the door. She was barefoot, in crumpled gray sweatpants and a tiny top, as if she'd just gotten out of bed. She looked morose and unwashed.

"Hi," she said. "You're back."

She didn't seem surprised to see him in her kitchen, almost as if she had been hoping he'd show up to rescue her. At least this is how he interpreted her lack of concern. This emboldened him.

"There's something I wanted to talk to you about before I left here."

"Then let's go talk outside." Ignoring her parents, she moved briskly across the room and walked out in the yard.

Andor made half a bow in their direction, as they were standing still, unable to decipher what was happening.

He had to be fast—he knew she wasn't going to be easily impressed and would give him only a few minutes. He said he'd be happy to give her a ride north so she could save money and still meet her friends if she wanted, but on the way he intended to make her a proposal. A well-paid job. A fun one, that involved traveling, possibly abroad as well. Then she could choose whether to follow her friends and go to France or take the opportunity he was offering her.

"Why don't you tell me now what kind of a job it is?" the girl asked.

He could see both her parents standing stiffly by the door, their necks stretched in the attempt to catch his words.

"It's complicated. We'll talk in the car."

The girl looked above his head into the distance, as if he didn't exist. She was beautiful in a way that was hard to see now—in those ugly clothes, without any makeup—but he would bring it out if she'd let him.

He thought it might be useful to put a little pressure on her.

"Think about it, but if you are interested, we need to get going. I've got people waiting for me farther north."

The girl shrugged. She pushed away a stone with the tips of her bare toes.

"Okay. I need a little time to pack my bag."

He controlled himself and repressed a smile.

"Sure."

He was hoping for a sign of recognition, a little spark in her eyes now that she'd agreed to leave with him, but the girl didn't change her sullen expression. She began to move away toward the house.

Andor called her.

"Hey!"

She turned around.

"I realized I don't even know your name," he said.

"It's Ada."

She didn't ask his.

It took her only half an hour to get ready.

The father was sitting in the kitchen smoking a cigarette, his back against the wall. The mother was drying pots and pans with a dishcloth. "Who is this man? Where is he taking you?" she asked the girl when she came into the room with her bag.

"He's giving me a job."

The father snickered and clicked his tongue with disgust.

"What's that supposed to mean?" the girl scolded him. She knew what they were thinking.

"Are you coming back?" the mother asked.

"Does it matter to you?"

She swore to herself this was the last time she'd see them. She wasn't going to call them ever again, no matter what.

The parents didn't come out to the old station wagon to say goodbye, didn't wave from the door. Ada threw her canvas bag in the backseat and hopped in. She pointed at the large wooden crates and asked what they were.

"I'll tell you later," Andor said with a hint of smugness as he started the engine.

————

Just before they reached Bari, Andor parked the car at a gas station. He turned to Ada, who had been quiet along the way, dozing off from time to time.

"Okay. Before I tell you what this job is about, I need to show you what's inside the boxes."

Ada yawned, stretching.

"I need to pee."

She seemed to be always dictating what needed to be done next, which was unnerving. Even now, just as he was about to unveil his pièce de résistance, she wasn't paying attention. He gestured toward the tiny market next to the gas pump.

"Okay, the restroom is inside. I'll wait for you here."

She came back after a few minutes, with her hair completely wet, dripping on her clothes. She must've put her head under the sink. He pointed at one of the wooden trunks.

"Open it," he said. "But go slowly and be gentle."

The girl fiddled with the lock. She peered inside.

The snakes were slithering, one on top of the other, in a sort of triple knot that did and undid itself in slow motion. The mix of colors was startling: the bright green of the anaconda, like fresh grass, mixed with the pale orange of the ball python and the dusty pink of the young rosy boa. Tails, tongues, scales, crossed over one another in a glossy tangle. She watched, enraptured.

"You can touch them—they are harmless."

She looked at him, and it seemed to Andor that she was waiting for his encouragement.

"Go on. You can hold one. Just be careful not to grab it by the head."

She placed her hand on the green anaconda. She seemed uncertain.

"Yes, like that. Now hold his body up with both hands."

She held the snake as if she were holding a rope at both

ends, then she lifted them slowly, so the snake was in front of her eyes. She grinned.

"It's cold."

Andor noticed how her voice had changed, had dropped its harsh timbre.

"Yes. And can you feel how strong it is?"

"Yes. It's like holding a . . ." She laughed. "An iron bar."

He saw how she was amused, but also intent, as she tested the firmness of those twitching muscles with her fingertips; he knew exactly what she felt, because anybody who had ever held a snake had the same sensation. Yes, it was like holding a giant dick with a hard-on, but it was also much more than that.

She wasn't afraid; that was the beautiful thing.

"And what's inside that one?" Ada asked, pointing her chin toward the larger trunk.

"A much bigger snake. Better not to let her out in the car. I'll show her to you later—if you'll be willing to work with me."

———

Ada burst out laughing when he told her about the circus. It was like a joke, she said. Wasn't it every parent's nightmare? A girl running away with the circus?

They were sitting at a Formica table inside the service station in front of two beers and slices of congealed pizza.

"Why a joke? I've worked with the circus for twenty-five years. I'm a professional," he said, seemingly hurt by her sarcasm. "It's a wonderful way of life. We are artists. Performers of the highest class. We come from different parts of the world and we're also a very close-knit family. You can be part of it too. My previous assistant has left and I need a new partner for my show."

He had become very serious. For the first time Ada felt he had some authority, after all. Maybe she had underestimated him because of the badly dyed hair and the flashy clothes.

"What kind of a show?"

Andor waved his manicured hand.

"Now it's called the Bandhra Fakhir. I come out in a Rajasthani outfit with a turban and my assistant has to pull out the snakes one by one from the boxes, going from small to big, while I play a flute like a snake charmer and she dances with them. The Burmese python comes out last—that's the grand finale of the show—and it curls all around her body. It's seven feet long and the audience always goes wild at that point because they think it's a constrictor."

"Is it dangerous?"

"Oh, no! I've had my snakes for many years. They are all used to being touched, and they are very gentle. The Burmese python, especially. She's the one inside the large box. Her name is Snow—she's an albino."

Andor was getting more and more excited.

"Wait till you see her. She's a beauty."

Something clicked off again in Ada's eyes. "What's the pay?"

"Food and shelter, plus thirty thousand lira per performance. You won't have any extra expenses."

Ada hesitated, uncertain.

"I've never been in a show. I mean . . . in front of an audience."

"That's not a problem at all. I can teach you in one afternoon. Basically all you have to do is dance to the music and learn how to handle the snakes."

"But I'm not a dancer . . ."

"It doesn't matter, Ada—you just have to come forward, moving your hips in rhythm. I'm sure you can do that, can't you? Think of belly dancing . . . or of any ancient, beautiful dance. All you have to do is look confident and exotic—the snakes do the rest. It's terrific, I promise you. The crowds go crazy. It's very, very exciting."

More than terrific, the description of the Bandhra act sounded vulgar and somewhat pathetic, but the idea of handling snakes excited her. It was a great story that would impress anybody. And besides, she was always looking for ways to make some money.

————

That same night they stopped in a motel near Canosa, on the edge of the Tavoliere plain, in northern Puglia. Andor asked for two single rooms right away, and Ada was relieved. She had expected him to linger at the concierge and find a lame excuse to get a double. She'd already planned a way to extricate herself—she wasn't going to have sex with him; that was a given, and besides, she knew how to defend herself in certain situations, had learned that in her days of traveling and hitchhiking on her own—but Andor's propriety pleased her.

She helped him carry both crates up to his room. He closed the door and sat on the floor, next to the big trunk.

He fiddled with the lock, and winked at Ada as he opened the lid. Ada gasped as Snow raised her head slowly, her body a luminous pattern of pure white and gold that grew thicker in the middle, till it became as large as one of Ada's thighs. Ada glanced at Andor expectantly and he nodded in return as if to give her permission to touch the snake. Ada moved her hand cautiously, until she brushed Snow's scales with her fingertips. She noticed how smooth and slippery they were to the touch—like silk, she thought—and again she felt the same incredible firmness, pure energy packed into an abstract shape. Most of the python's body was still curled up in knots, each coil sliding in a different direction in the attempt to unfurl, so that inside the trunk there seemed to be more than just one snake. She tried to hold Snow around the middle, where her body was the thickest, but she couldn't clasp her fingers around it—it was way too large. She looked again at Andor, exhilarated.

"She's so heavy, I can hardly lift her!"

He laughed. It was lovely to see her genuine enthusiasm.

"She weighs about ten kilos; she's just a baby. She will weigh four or five times that once she grows."

Snow was indeed like a fantasy—a creature from a fairy tale, a beautiful monster fabricated in a dream—and yet there she was, so real and alive, moving under the touch of Ada's fingertips.

"You can do it," he said. "You are a natural."

"How do you know that?" Ada asked, and for the first time she felt she could maybe trust this strange man, so unlike any person she would ever consider taking up with.

Andor didn't answer. Instead he just extended his hand.

"So? Is this a done deal? Are we partners now?"

Ada took his hand and shook it.

———

Later, after they had something to eat in a small trattoria across the street, they went back upstairs to the room and Andor opened a duffel bag, pulling out a tangle of shiny fabrics.

"These belonged to Zara, my ex-assistant. They might be big on you but we can have them fixed."

There was a full bayadere costume, with a golden bra and embroidered harem pants in a semi-sheer material, a tiny black and silver top, a full pleated skirt in bright green and red stripes that sat low on the hips. There were anklets with tiny bells attached, gaudy earrings made of plastic and chunky bracelets studded with fake gems. She kept pulling out these small treasures one by one, mystified.

"What are these?"

"These are the costumes we used on the show. But if you like, we can have some new ones made for you. I'm thinking of maybe doing something different, with more of a modern feel to it. But for now these will do. Try them on."

The thought of undressing in front of him bothered her, but deep down she knew that all those offerings must come with a price. She wasn't particularly prudish, had no problem taking off her clothes in front of her friends—they had spent months in Greece, all of them naked on the beach—but showing her tits in front of an older man was a different matter.

"Take them to your room and try them on," Andor said.

"Let me know tomorrow if they fit you or they need to be altered."

Ada smelled the costumes. He'd had them cleaned, and she wondered whether he had done it for her. She folded the clothes neatly one by one.

They were hers now. She'd take good care of them.

———

After long stretches of golden wheat fields rolling past the window, the road began to climb through low, undulating green hills and then into the mountains of Irpinia. The weather changed. The sun disappeared behind the heavy clouds and it was suddenly cold and rainy, as if they had stepped into winter in the course of only a few hours. Tall pines shrouded the side of the mountain and the landscape seemed to Ada sadder and somehow ominous.

Just before the entrance to a town called Grottaminarda, Andor turned into a large parking lot. The green circus tent was pitched right there, across from a crummy supermarket: a smaller affair than Ada had expected. Caravans and rusty trucks were parked behind the building in the midst of a muddy field beside a deserted playground. Tiny colorful flags tied to the tent's ropes flapped in the wind; half-ripped posters on the wall of the parking lot shouted in bold red and purple letters WEISSER CIRCUS—ALL THE WAY FROM GERMANY! A blurry photo showed a trainer holding a whip, tigers jumping through a fire ring. Ada was silent and seemed deflated somehow. Andor wished they'd arrived on a sunnier afternoon, when there were more people around, music blaring from the speakers.

"It's a family circus, more intimate. You'll see, it's a real fun way of living," he said.

Ada didn't respond. She kept her eyes on the derelict playground and the windswept field. Andor tried to sound joyful as he began to unload the boxes near his caravan.

"We should start right away. We have only a couple of days of rehearsals. I want you to be ready to start next week."

———

Ada felt better the minute she stepped inside Andor's caravan. It was another world in there: it had a living room with carpets, a red sofa and armchairs. There was a large bedroom, a kitchenette and a bathroom with a small bathtub. There were books piled up here and there, lots of pictures stacked on the walls, embroidered and fringed lampshades, cushions and bright curtains made from Indian fabrics. It was cozy, colorful, like rooms she had seen only in the old Hollywood movies she loved.

"You can sleep on the sofa," Andor said casually, as he carried a couple of suitcases.

"Where is everybody else?" she asked.

"It's our day off today. Probably sleeping or watching TV inside their caravans. Or maybe getting drunk at the village bar. Who knows."

Later that same night Andor asked her to try on the clothes he had given her. He then combed and tightened her long hair in a bun, like he would do with a child, gently lined her eyes with a black pencil, applied rouge on her cheeks and red on her lips, then picked each piece of jewelry from the duffel bag and clasped it to her neck, ankles and wrists. No one had ever done anything like this to her. For a fleeting moment her mind went back to her sister on her wedding day: how she had been attended by so many hands in order to complete her transformation. How she had walked down the aisle made up like a doll, with her hair curled into a stiff pyramid, her body constricted in a polyester gown bursting at the seams. Ada looked at herself in a full-length mirror. The heavy makeup aged her too, and the clothes looked cheap and a tad sleazy, but she didn't mind: what she was meant to do was just play a part, like an actress onstage, under the lights. Her life still belonged to her, and to her only.

Ada started out handling the smaller snakes first, and pretty soon she got the gist of it. She let them slide along her arms and shoulders, slither around her waist like a belt. The tight grip of the snakes, as they twirled around her body, gave her a jolt of excitement. Now she was dancing slowly around the room, with her eyes half closed, to the sound of music booming from the portable stereo. When the music stopped she did a little shimmying dance of triumph. Andor clapped, ecstatic.

"When can I handle Snow?" she asked. Her eyes were glowing now.

"Tomorrow we can start practicing with her in the ring. We need more space than this room. That baby's a big one."

———

The following week, in front of the audience—mainly local families from the nearby villages who had come by the hundreds—they perfected and improved their act until they could do it with their eyes closed. Andor appeared onstage playing a flute, as Ada, hidden in one of the trunks, slowly emerged. By then Ada was sufficiently at ease with the snakes, and she didn't mind lying with them in the dark for a handful of seconds. She slid out of the trunk and danced around the ring, holding the smaller python and the green anaconda above her head. There were gasps and whispers, ooohs and aaahs from the children. The minute the excitement began to wane, Ada lifted the lid of the larger trunk, as Andor had instructed her, and stretched out her arm, as an invitation. The audience gasped as Snow's head and thick body arose, erect. Under the bright lights Snow's white and golden skin was almost blinding. The Burmese python came slowly out of the box, and all her seven feet began to climb upon Ada's extended arm, reaching her shoulder, her back, twirling around her body as if on a pole. People from the audience began to scream. At this point Ada lay down and pretended to be gasping for air. Snow knew to curl around her torso and her neck, but never to tighten her grip. This was Ada's favorite moment of the show. Not only because the audience went crazy as the music reached a frenzied pitch, but because in the few minutes before Andor mimicked her rescue and the number came to the end, she was at her closest with Snow; it was their most intimate time. She felt Snow's cold scales pressing against her skin. It was better than being stoned, to be able to allow that embrace without fear. The knowledge that her body had become a familiar territory for this incredible creature, who by now knew her shape and smell so intimately, who would never hurt her, and the feeling that within their embrace some kind of amazing, magical energy was exchanged: she couldn't name it, but it was like an electric shock, even a revelation.

Maybe she had never known she had a power. Maybe she was an otherworldly creature herself.

———

The days had a pretty late start in the circus; everyone liked to sleep in and nothing happened before ten or eleven. There were animals to feed—a few horses, a couple of camels, a small Sri Lankan elephant, two aging tigers—numbers to rehearse, the tent to clean up and prepare for the next show. Despite its name, nobody in the Weisser Circus came from Germany. Most of the performers were from Eastern Europe, Romania and Hungary; only a few of them spoke some Italian, and none as fluently as Andor.

After only a few days Ada had fallen half in love with the four sisters from the Flying Hawks acrobatic number. In the early afternoons she sneaked inside the empty ring, sat on a hay bale and watched them practice. The girls were tiny, barely five feet, but they were precision machines; even when they were just standing still, they had a way of adhering to the ground that made them look as if they were made of steel. They did a quick warm-up routine of handstands and push-ups, and when they climbed the ladder up to the trapeze and began to swing, hanging by one leg, catching each other's hands in midair and shimmering under the spotlights, they looked twice the size.

Ada's infatuation wasn't reciprocated. The girls showed no interest in her; in fact they hardly said hello. Ada was aware there must be a hierarchy—it was one thing to risk your life flying on a trapeze or working with tigers—and clearly dancing with snakes didn't impress anybody. But it wasn't just that. The circus people had greeted her without enthusiasm. Nobody was hostile, not the clowns, not the magician, not the elephant trainer or the horse riders. But she was invisible to most of them, because in Romany culture she was a *gadji*, an outsider.

"It'll take a little time. At the beginning I also had to win their trust, because I'm Hungarian," Andor reassured her. "Although they've lived in Hungary for five centuries they still think of themselves as Romany. And they like to keep to themselves."

———

It was nearly October. One could feel the fall in the change of light: the sky had taken on a hue of darker blue, and the early-morning sun projected starker shadows on the ground. There were a few more dates farther west for the circus to perform before it closed down for the winter. The towns they toured seemed desolate, the streets badly lit at night, weather-stained buildings covered in graffiti, cracked pavement, an air of abandonment and despair. The audiences were beginning to thin out as the days got shorter. By then Ada had taken full charge of the snakes. She cleaned their boxes every day, fed them live chicks when it was possible to find them or else bought small frozen rodents in the pet shops of the larger towns and watched them being swallowed. Nothing deterred her.

———

It didn't take very long for Ada to move from the sofa to Andor's bed. She did it without thinking, almost out of courtesy at first, or because at times she felt lonely, but soon it became natural and she never looked back.

Among the pictures stacked on the wall she studied a few that looked as though they were taken ten or twenty years earlier, now bleached by sunlight and curled at the corners. Apparently, Andor had been a trapeze artist himself before he switched to snakes. There he was, an attractive, bare-chested young man in sparkly leggings with a cascade of dark hair reaching his shoulders, showing off his abs. Ada could, with a slight effort, still recognize faint traces of that younger body showing beneath the shape of his calves, his biceps, his muscular thighs. But there were differences too: he had a belly now and his skin was sagging in funny places. Whenever they had sex Ada tried not to notice too much how he had aged compared to the photos. Sometimes she just closed her eyes and in his place she pictured the trapeze artist he once was. Because his lovemaking was kind and never selfish, she found a release that calmed her down and afterward she slept soundly next to him. This was the very first time she felt looked after. Sex seemed a way of giving something in return.

———

It was her birthday, she had been on the road for almost three months already and she felt the urge to hear a familiar voice.

Ada wanted to talk to Teresa, but she didn't have her phone number now that her sister was married and living somewhere else with her husband. She called her parents from a public phone in Nola, a smaller town not far from Naples. Her mother answered. Ada could hear the television in the background and she immediately conjured up the kitchen, its smell of garlic and stale breath. She asked for her sister's number.

"What do you need it for?" the mother asked with spite. "She's not going to want to talk to you anyway. You have disgraced us all."

"What now? What have I done?"

"You and that man. The whole town has seen you."

Apparently, a small local TV channel had broadcast a short clip of the Weisser Circus. Everyone had recognized her, belly dancing half naked with snakes coiling around her, like a witch, her mother said, a pervert, a slut.

Ada hung up.

———

Each night Andor slid into his bed with a thumping heart.

He had known from the very first day that eventually she'd gain trust and would come to him. He just had to make sure she'd feel safe and comfortable every step of the way. It was a long process, and each day she got imperceptibly closer, but he knew the drill: he had tamed creatures far more suspicious or recalcitrant. Despite this certainty, when she'd opened up at last, he still couldn't believe he had won her over. That he could so easily hold her, enter her, that she'd allow him to kiss every part of her body as if it now belonged to him. Sometimes he would've liked to rest his head on her breast, release the knot in his throat—maybe even cry a little—and tell her how much he loved her.

In the mornings, as soon as she woke up, Ada invariably put on the same mask and showed the same detached indifference as the girl he had met under the fig tree. Andor knew it wasn't her fault and she couldn't help it; he could sense there was loss inside her. It was a cold, hollow space nobody had ever attended to. Unloved children grew into emotional illiterates, he well knew that, and to a degree it was that emptiness that had attracted him in the first place. He had the power to replenish it, if only she'd allow him. With time, with patience, he kept repeating to himself.

Since he had brought Ada to the circus, he too had been mildly ostracized. He was no longer invited to visit the others at night, to drink or play cards in their caravan. Not that he cared. He was more well-read than most of them and had a degree in languages, and by now he had spent so many years in their company that he felt ready for a drastic change. But he did worry about Ada. He had promised her she'd find a family within the circus, but instead now he too had been shunned.

Ada didn't seem to mind too much the lack of company. She could spend a big chunk of the day lying on the red couch, sometimes reading a book, drifting into and out of sleep, unwrapping the chocolates that he bought for her. She would crumple the golden foil into tiny balls and flick them away. Sometimes he'd find tiny specks of gold behind the cushions or under the bedsheets.

But every night, in the ring, no matter how small an audience, he saw how Ada was revived from her lethargy. She emerged from the trunk as if from the dead, the snakes curling around her arms like shiny bangles, her eyes glowing, her cheeks flushed with color. Andor looked at the same miracle take place every night, this transfiguration that he had orchestrated.

I gave her a new life, he said to himself. I've taken her by the hand and I've led her to her true nature. It's a miracle of beauty, and she doesn't even know it's happening.

———

Ada had heard about the tarot reader.

Nadya, the mother of the Flying Hawks sisters, used to be a trapeze artist but she no longer performed because of a bad neck injury. These days she performed a solo dressage act, riding one of the Arabian horses, which danced to a music-box tune. She also appeared in the final parade, on top of the white horse, all dressed up in sequins and a bright-red feather headdress.

"Is she any good?" Ada asked Andor.

"I don't know. I'm the only one here who has never had a reading. Everyone else says she's incredible."

"Why didn't you?"

He shrugged.

"Who wants to know the future? Not me."

But Ada did. There was so much future stretching ahead of her, shrouding its content in a white fog. Her life was bound to change again and again and again, there were so many more doors to be opened, like a sequence of rooms leading one into the next. New landscapes, new faces to be seen. Who wouldn't want to peek through that fog? Taste what was waiting ahead?

She looked at Andor with pity. His life had already been mapped out. She might be the last surprise he would ever come across. No wonder he wasn't keen to find out how little was left for him after she'd be gone.

The Flying Hawks caravan smelled of strong detergents. It was messy, cluttered, with lots of mirrors hanging on the walls, dusty plastic flowers scattered in ugly vases, two big dolls dressed in synthetic lace propped on the couch. Nadya was intent on scrubbing the kitchenette wearing bright-yellow plastic gloves. She sure looked different without the makeup and the feathers. More like a regular housewife in a slackened sweatsuit, with darker roots showing under the bleached hair, her face reddish around her nose, eyelids drooping underneath overplucked eyebrows. In a corner of the small room, the oldest of the daughters, in a skimpy dress, was sprawled on an armchair, listening to her Walkman with earphones, her muscular leg beating the tempo on the armrest. She hadn't bothered to turn her head to greet Andor and Ada when they walked in.

Andor spoke to Nadya in Hungarian—or was it Czech, Serbian, Polish? Ada couldn't tell; all those guttural languages sounded pretty much the same to her. Nadya kept answering with short nasal grunts. She pulled off her gloves and wiped her hands on her hips. She pointed at a small table.

"She says she can do the reading now if you want. Is that okay?" Andor said to Ada. Something was bothering him, she could tell.

"Yes. That's great."

"Okay, then, let's sit down. I'll have to translate," he said, evidently annoyed.

"No. I don't want you in here," Ada said.

Andor opened his arms, exasperated.

"But how will you understand?"

Ada stared at him fiercely.

"It's not your business. This is private."

"You go now," Nadya said to Andor in Italian, indicating the door. He turned around without saying another word.

Droopy shoulders, Ada thought, as she watched him walk away.

———

Nadya began to shuffle the cards. It was an old pack, the cards' edges curling, their surface oily, like banknotes that had changed too many hands. With a single, skillful move, she spread them facedown in a fan shape and said something in her language, showing her five fingers.

"I pick five cards?" Ada asked, and she nodded.

Ada floated her hand on top of the cards, hovering it in midair, as if waiting for a magnetic force to guide her. She felt a shift, a thickening of the air inside the stuffy room—everything including her breath was denser, scintillating. Yes, something was definitely about to happen. Then she began to pick one card at a time as if her life depended on it.

Nadya placed each card facedown in a cross. She flipped the one in the center. It showed a handsome young man in a chariot led by two sphinxes. Ada realized the girl on the armchair had removed the earphones and was now listening to them.

Nadya stared at the card, then spoke quickly without lifting her eyes from the table. Her Italian was stilted but rather good.

"You are being pressured in a situation by someone. You are not very happy. Maybe a little bit but not entirely. You must move forward," she said, and placed her finger on the Chariot card. "This means moving away, into new life."

Ada nodded, pretending this piece of information was unimportant and it didn't affect her in any way. Actually, it bothered her that the other girl had decided she was more interested in the tarots than in her music. Ada encouraged Nadya to disclose the next card.

A man with a crown. Nadya made an approving sound, as if that were the card she had been waiting for: a king. This couldn't possibly be a bad thing, Ada thought. Nadya tilted her head and tapped on the card pensively, then she started talking almost to herself.

"Yes, the Emperor. You see this? Older man. He's probably in love with you. This is the pressure the Chariot is showing. This man want to bind you to him; maybe he is very lonely."

Ada felt uneasy. Had this been a good idea? Was the girl going to laugh behind her back with her sisters, with the rest of the circus people?

But Nadya was already flipping the next card. It showed two dogs howling at the moon. Nadya stared at it, tapped her fingertips very lightly on it—doubtful for a few seconds, then she spoke again.

"The Moon. This means confusion. You are not telling yourself truth about current situation. Maybe you are depressed and you don't know. Maybe this is because of Emperor?"

Ada shrugged dismissively, as if she had no idea what the cards might be referring to. But Nadya seemed to be getting more excited, as if the picture were finally coming together. She turned the next card.

"Ha!" Nadya slapped the card with a joyful expression. Two figures, a man and a woman with flower garlands in their hair, were holding two cups next to each other in a toast. They looked beautiful. And young.

"Two of cups! New partner is coming into your life. Maybe a friend, maybe a lover. This partner will influence your destiny. It will bring happiness and trust."

Ada looked at the tarot reader's daughter. She caught a flash of recognition in her eyes at last. A hint of a smile. Nadya said a word in her language and repeated it a couple of times.

"She says this is very good," the Flying Hawks girl said languidly from her armchair.

"Okay. That's nice," Ada said. "When?"

Nadya tapped forcefully on the card twice.

"Soon. Very soon."

Then she turned up the last card. It was a man hanging upside down from a tree. Ada frowned.

"Wow. Is this bad?"

Nadya shook her head vigorously. She spoke quickly. The girl nodded.

"Hanged man is change. Old must die to create the new. You leave this situation. Soon, in the next future. That is very good."

————

Nadya had refused to be paid for the reading and said something to the daughter. The daughter repressed a grin, plugged the earphones back in and returned to her music. Outside it had started to drizzle.

Ada stepped down from the caravan and saw the rest of the Flying Hawks sisters heaped together on top of a couple of big trunks under a tarpaulin. They were eating something with their hands from the same plate. They stared at Ada without waving. They looked like a cluster of newborn puppies, close as they were to one another in a tangle of bare arms and feet.

"Who the fuck cares," Ada whispered under her breath as she walked away briskly. She wasn't sure whether she meant she didn't care about the reading, or about not having sisters she could hang out and eat from the same plate with.

———

In November the circus closed down for the season.

The morning after the last show in Sant'Agata dè Goti, a small town in the Apennine Mountains, Ada walked to the grandstand and watched as Andor and a few other men began to unhook the rigging. The ringmaster, the uncle of the Flying Hawks girls, had climbed the center pole and was yelling instructions to the men below, each one of them knowing exactly what to do, when to pull or loosen the ropes and the hooks until, hours later, the tent lay flat on the ground like a dead beast and was folded and stored in the spool truck.

The circus shows would resume by the end of March. Meanwhile, Andor told her, the two of them could use the downtime to rest. He made it sound like a pleasant opportunity and told her he would take care of her food and small expenses so that she wouldn't have to touch any of the money she had saved. He also said that they could come up with ideas for a new act, and that he'd been thinking about a sort of *Indi-*

ana Jones theme. He was to dress in a khaki outfit, complete with Stetson hat and cowboy boots, like the character from the films and she could be his American partner. Wouldn't she like to play a strong woman, an archaeologist or maybe an explorer?

She winced. "That's so silly," she said. "Plus I don't want to wear safari clothes. I prefer to stick to my old costumes."

Andor immediately backtracked. "Okay, no problem. Then you can be the goddess of the Temple of Doom or something. In any case I'm open to suggestions."

———

There were going-away parties and farewells as a good number of the performers went back to their homes in Eastern Europe. Andor said this happened every year at the beginning of winter: many left, to return again in the early spring, and only a few remained, those who had no real home to go back to. Ada watched through strips of rain as people packed up and loaded their cars, leaving at the break of dawn. Over the next few days more and more of them left. Then suddenly one day it all went quiet. Even the snakes had gone into hibernation.

Those who had chosen to stay moved the trucks with the animals and the remaining trailers to a cornfield in a nondescript town near Salerno, inland from the Amalfi Coast, where the mayor had given them permission to settle and camp during the cold months for a small fee.

Ada was confused: without the tent, the circus was no longer a circus, but a bunch of rusty trailers. Other than feeding and taking care of the animals, there was not much going on during the day. The Flying Hawks had left, and with them most of the top artists. She missed the grandstand, the feeling of being underneath the protection of the tent, the echo, the lights, the smell of sawdust mixed with sweat and rosin.

Above all, she missed Snow and the other snakes, she realized, the feel of their muscles on her bare skin.

———————

The Iranians arrived on a sunny December morning. Ada sat up from the red couch where she was eating her chocolates and watched them through the frosted window as they drove inside the camping ground, a procession of white Mercedes cars followed by a couple of large trailers. She crumpled the umpteenth golden foil and walked out the door. She sat on the step.

The cold *tramontana* wind that blows from the north had swept off the dampness of the November rains. The air was fragrant; one could smell the freshness of snow already falling up in the distant mountains. Ada closed her eyes, letting the winter sun warm up her skin.

The men were unpacking their belongings, unrolling carpets, pulling out cushions from the car trunks. Andor followed Ada outside and stood next to her on the step.

"A bunch of crooks," he said with contempt. "They will bring trouble."

She turned to him, irked.

"How do you know that? Sometimes you sound like such an old fart."

Those men didn't seem like they were looking to steal anything. Their cars and clothes were expensive, their hair was black, long and shiny, they were handsome. And they were young.

————

At night, beside him, she had turned into a corpse. He didn't even try to touch her, knowing that once he was overtly rejected it would set a precedent and she might migrate back to the red sofa. He needed her body to be near his, at least at night, because during the day she was gone most of the time. But even so he knew she was no longer there, and because they had never spoken about what their sexual relationship was or what it meant, he felt helpless and unable to ask her what had gone wrong.

Every morning, as soon as Ada saw the young Iranians move around the camp, preparing tea, washing clothes, she would run out.

The women had no problems befriending her; they didn't treat her as a stranger. Like the men, the women had long hair but theirs fell down to their waists and their eyes were lined with kohl. Some of them were pregnant, some already had a couple of babies, but they were only a few years older than Ada. They laughed with her, invited her to sit with them and offered to put henna in her hair. They insisted they must wax her entire body with a mixture of honey and sugar. One day Andor found a bunch of them sitting with Ada on the floor of the caravan, going through the costumes of the Bandhra Fakhir act. Ada let them borrow whatever they liked—the harem pants, the sparkling silver top, the Rajasthani skirt. Soon Ada started looking like one of them. She let her hair loose, she took to wearing sandals even though it was nearly Christmas. Andor seemed not to mind; after all Ada deserved some company, and it was okay if she imitated their style.

The men were friendly as well. They spoke some English, and it turned out that Ada knew a few words and had no problem making herself understood. Now, as soon as it got dark, she disappeared into one of their trailers, and Andor imagined her cross-legged on the thick carpets that lined the floor. He pictured her resting on the pillows, drinking the dark tea the women served, smoking hashish with them. He was never invited to join them.

"I know those people smoke drugs. They do it in front of everybody—it's no big secret," he said to Ada one morning while making coffee on the camping stove of the caravan. She had just taken a shower and had tied a sarong around her body. Her legs were still damp and glistened with tiny drops.

Ada had told him she had had a problem with using drugs in the past, and that had come as a surprise to Andor. She didn't like talking about it, yet once, in passing, she mentioned the fact she had never touched a needle in her life.

Ada shrugged and flipped her wet hair over her head, then began to dry it with a towel.

"It worries me," he said.

But Ada ignored him, still bending over, massaging her head.

"You've been so good—you should stay away from people who use hashish and God knows what else."

Ada straightened up and threw the towel on the floor. She sighed impatiently.

"Oh, great. Are you going to be tailing me now? All I need is for you to become a policeman, like my father."

———

There was one man in particular. He had fine hands with slender fingers and wore his long hair parted in the middle. He seemed to be the leader of the group despite his young age. He was joyous, almost childish at times. Andor kept watching him from a distance, and he noticed the way he joked with the other men, how women were in awe of him. Once Andor crossed paths with him on the way to the water pipe where they filled their cans. The man greeted him politely and Andor decided not to return the courtesy. But he caught a glimpse of his eyes: they were yellow, like a cat's.

Each night Ada came back to the caravan too tired to talk, her hair smelling of tobacco and hashish. True, Ada had always been quiet, but her silence now was of a different kind; it was lifeless, as if she were no longer there. She undressed quickly, got into bed and turned her back to Andor. Each sleepless night he rehearsed a new speech, cautiously selecting the words for questions that needed to be answered. Each morning he lost heart and didn't dare open his mouth.

It was already late in the day and he was washing the previous night's dishes, when she came out of the bedroom, her hair still in a braid, her face puffy from too much sleep. He noticed a blue dot on her cheekbone.

"What's that?" he asked.

"Nothing."

He stood up and seized her arm with uncanny strength. Ada tried to wriggle out of his grasp, but Andor wouldn't let her go.

"Who did this to you?"

"What do you care? Leave me alone."

He got closer, his warm breath on her face. She looked scared for the first time. He pressed his fingers on her cheekbone, in an attempt to remove the spot.

"You know what this means?"

"It's nothing. It means nothing. It's just a tattoo."

He was seething with rage, his breathing shortened.

"Who did it?"

"What's the point? You don't know his name, you don't even know who he is."

But he did. And before he knew it, he'd slapped her face.

"Gypsies give this tattoo to married women, you fucking idiot. He marked you. That's what it means!"

Ada was still in shock. He had never used language like that, or touched her with less than kindness. She yelled back, but her voice was strangled, weaker.

"Don't you dare touch me again!"

"I'm sorry, I . . ." He too was in shock that he had hit her.

She interrupted him: "And stop calling them Gypsies! You know nothing! They fled, escaped a repressive regime. Don't you know that even music is banned in Iran? Anything Western is illegal there!"

"Repressive regime? Ha!" he exclaimed with disdain. "Since when have you become an expert on Iranian politics?"

He was tired of losing, of being afraid. He shook her by the shoulders.

"They're drug addicts, Ada. Did they make you smoke opium too? I bet they did!"

But the more heated his rage, the less it seemed to affect Ada. She had regained her composure and was staring at him coldly now, as though she had retreated inside a protected zone where nothing could touch her. Andor sensed that she was slipping away fast, but he pushed himself. He had to pretend he still possessed her.

"Tomorrow I'm taking you to someone to erase this tattoo."

She looked gravely at him. There was a silence. Then she spoke calmly.

"Tomorrow they are leaving and I'm going with them."

Ada would leave that very night, after collecting her few things.

She didn't bother to take what was left of her costumes; she wouldn't need them. But before leaving she did need to do one last thing, and she didn't want Andor to see. She waited for him to leave the trailer and then rushed to the end of the caravan where the trunks had been stowed away. She opened the largest one. And there she was, Snow, curled up in her winter sleep. Ada leaned in and moved her hand along the snake's spine, then kissed her white scales. Snow's body felt still, as if it had lost all power, and was as cold as a corpse.

"*Adieu,* my love," she whispered, closing her eyes for a moment.

———

Andor is sitting in his small apartment in Budapest.

He's retired and he has aged. He now lives on a meager state pension and gets some help from his daughter, Hanna, who was conceived when he was still a young trapeze artist. He's been an estranged father for most of her life, but lately their relationship, although complicated—and thanks to Hanna's years of therapy—has improved. She's in her early forties and lives in Barcelona with her husband and their little boy.

Andor visits her two or three times a year. These reunions have become a habit, one they both have learned to enjoy. Because of their long-distance relationship Hanna has just persuaded Andor to open a Facebook account. He has agreed, reluctantly—it seems childish for a man of his age to be asking for friendship from people he has lost touch with. Today, only his second day on Facebook, he has figured out more or less how the whole thing works.

He has just typed in Ada's name, and is looking at the photos on her page.

There she is, no longer the girl he knew, now close to fifty. She's cut her hair shorter—it's lightly sprayed with gray now—and she wears flat shoes and nicely cut dresses. Apparently she lives somewhere in Scotland, with a man and two tall girls who look more like the father; he's quite tall and handsome, with light-blond hair and a short beard. He could be a journalist, or maybe a professor, because of the round glasses and that casual, bookish look. Ada's profile says she now works as a production designer with a theater company in Edinburgh. Andor is pleased; surely the atmosphere of the Weisser Circus left an imprint on her. It matters to him that the brief life they shared may have inspired her to find her calling.

Andor cannot believe he can peek into her life with so much detail available to him. Here she is again, in a spacious living room filled with light, furnished with nice carpets and sofas. There is a dog too. It's a large white beast that looks like a wolf with blue eyes.

And here she and the blond man are on vacation some-where warm. It could be India, or Thailand. There is a beach and palm trees and she's in a bikini. The sight of her bare legs gives him a start. He knows them so well, the shape, the tex-ture of her calves. She and her husband still look fit—surely they must exercise, take classes in a gym, run, maybe do yoga or something, whereas his seventy-five-year-old body has given up after all the work it has been put through. Andor has gained too much weight, he has arthritis, he's lost his hair. What would Ada's husband think if he knew that his wife was the lover of such an old man? And would she recoil in shame if she saw him now?

But these are negative thoughts, and he doesn't like to dwell on them. Especially at his age, when one can count on two hands how much time one has left, he has made a rule never to indulge in regrets but to try to keep the focus on the bright side of things, the happy memories and whatnot. It's the only way, really.

He tried so hard to make her happy, to possess her (how foolish of him!), but in the end it was this blond man who soothed her and filled the emptiness that had made her so hard. Well, Andor thinks, he seems a nice man. It's good to know that Ada didn't get lost: she has a family, she has money, an artistic job, which, perhaps, in part she owes to him. He wonders whether she has reconciled with her parents back in the village.

Up in the right-hand corner there is a private message box he can click on.

Andor is surprised by how easily he composes his message; it's as though the words have been lodging inside him for God knows how long, exactly in that same order. But—he's not an impulsive man, after all—he reads it over and over, pruning it here and there.

Dear Ada: It's been so long! I'm so happy I found you at last. I see you are in Scotland, and you have a beautiful family. And what a beautiful house! Please send me your telephone number—I long to hear your voice. I also want to come and visit you—we have so much to talk about. Right now I'm unable to travel because I have a small cardiac problem, nothing to worry about, but I'm supposed to have an operation in a couple of weeks. I'll come visit when I feel strong again. The other day I went for a checkup and I told the surgeon that when he'll cut me open with the knife he has to pay attention because inside my heart he'll find a little girl curled up on a red sofa, nibbling on her chocolates. I warned him he must be very gentle, so he doesn't disturb her, because she's been living inside me for a very long time and I need her to stay there, and be happy and warm.

He looks once more at one of the photos. It's Ada in a close-up. In the back he can see a portion of a Christmas tree. Her face has gained a few lines but she still looks beautiful. No matter how domesticated her life seems now, Ada's eyes still retain the same glimmer he recognized when he first saw her under the fig tree, almost twenty-five years ago. That's how he knew, right away, that the girl must have a power.

He enlarges the image—his daughter has just shown him how to do that—because he needs to get real close.

And yes, it's still there. On her cheekbone, the blue dot.

ANIMAL SPIRIT

They arrived on the island after a long day of travel, when the sun was lowering and the light glorious. The house stood isolated, on the northern side of the island, in the middle of a golden field shadowed by oaks. A dirt path unfurled in the tall yellow grass all the way to a secluded beach. It was a three-minute walk from bedroom to water, they had read on the rental website, and that's when Clara said, "Let's take it, it's perfect, we can tumble out of bed and have a swim before breakfast. That's what I call a dream location." The property owner was a rich woman called Hera, like Zeus's wife—a detail they found amusing. Hera was an interior designer who lived in Athens and her island house was spartan and exquisite in its simplicity.

The housecleaner spoke a basic Italian; her name was Artemis—another reason for them to be delighted. She showed the four of them how to operate the light switches, the shower, the oven and the TV. When she finally left, they looked excitedly around the house, calling one another from room to room, pointing at each lovely detail: the outdoor shower hidden beneath a banana tree and a cluster of wild orchids, the hammock dangling under the shadow of the oaks, the fine linen sheets.

They were two couples in their mid-thirties: Carlos and Jacopo, who had known each other for a very long time; and Clara and Gabriel, who had met only a couple of months earlier. One couple had known each other for perhaps too long, the other shared no history. Both couples were bound to each other by tendrils that at times felt tenuous—one too worn out, the other too fresh——so that before leaving for the vacation they had been careful to mask whatever anxiety they felt.

Yet, once arrived at the house, each one felt secretly confident that Hera's house, the sun and the sea, Greece itself, would smooth whatever unease they felt.

————

Clara was in love with Gabriel.

A few days after she had made love to him for the first time she had dinner with Carlos and Jacopo, whom she considered her best friends. The idea had been to celebrate the fact that Clara had actually fallen in love after a long period of not wanting to fall in love. Carlos had prepared a delicious dinner for her and Jacopo in his cozy apartment. It was supposed to be a happy celebration, but when Clara turned up she was on the verge of tears.

Clara was a painter who felt she deserved more consideration. Although her work sold well—it wasn't expensive and its bold, bright colors looked good on the walls—prominent art critics often deemed her paintings too "decorative" and she was consistently ignored by the international art magazines. Somehow the suffering for this lack of recognition had become a recurrent theme in her life.

She had fallen in love with Gabriel so hard, she said, and now all she could see was disaster looming ahead. Eventually—she just knew it—Gabriel would break her heart. She said all this to Carlos and Jacopo while sitting cross-legged on the floor, puffing on a joint half drunk and picking at tiny morsels of Carlos's perfectly cooked *spaghetti alle vongole*.

"Two people fall in love and right away you've got a corpse right there," she said. "It's an unspoken agreement, but it's clear from the start which one of the two will be the killer and which will be the one to succumb. In order for love to work, one of the two has to pledge, 'I'm giving myself entirely to you—look, I'm ditching all my weapons,' and that's what I just did with Gabriel."

Carlos and Jacopo told her she was being melodramatic and she needed to relax.

"Just go slow, take one day at a time, like they tell people in AA," Jacopo said.

"And besides, there's no insurance anyone can buy against heartbreak," Carlos added.

"Holding back has never been my forte," Clara said. "I've just fallen for him. I actually nosedived."

What was so special about this man? the two asked.

"Two things. Number one, and I know this is going to sound superficial, he's my aesthetic ideal. The brooding Heathcliff type. I love everything about him, from his forearms and collarbone to his beautiful toes. My body just wants his, all the time."

"Beautiful toes?" Carlos asked. "Sounds promising. . . ."

"And number two?" Jacopo asked and then added, in a cajoling tone, "Perhaps something on a less superficial level?"

"I can't quite grasp what it is—we've only just started seeing each other—and he's guarded, he won't let anybody see through him. But I know there's something vulnerable and hurting inside, like an unloved child who's put up a shield. I just don't know if he'll ever allow me in. But I'm obsessed. I want to gain access."

"Don't push," Jacopo said.

"No, I don't want to fuck it up. But I wish I could say out loud, 'I love you, I'm crazy for you,' and maybe hear the same from him? Or be able to ask, 'Is this thing serious, or is it just sex with no strings attached?' "

After Clara left, Jacopo helped clear up the table and wash the dishes. He lived nearby, and he and Carlos were always at each other's places, eating or binge-watching TV series on the couch.

"It's early—you don't have to go yet," Carlos said, handing Jacopo rolling papers and the tin box where he kept his stash. He always found any excuse to keep his friends from calling it a night because he didn't fall asleep till very late. Carlos had a high-pressure job as an accessories designer for a major fashion brand and suffered from insomnia because of the constant stress and deadlines.

He and Jacopo sat on the couch and talked about Clara and her preoccupations while Jacopo rolled two joints on the low table. Clara had had various relationships in the past, none of which had ended well, and Carlos and Jacopo were concerned she would get hurt again. She showed her best side whenever in their company—funny, curious, engaging—but with men with whom she was involved romantically she too often became needy and demanding, reserving for them the tragic version of herself. It could get exhausting.

"When you add sex to the equation it's always exciting, but it creates a layer of stress, especially when you first meet someone," Carlos said.

He exhaled forcefully from the left side of his mouth, and cleared his voice.

"It's a good thing you and I don't have to go through that again."

When Carlos and Jacopo had first met, at a late-night party almost ten years earlier, they had sex the very same night, but right away Carlos realized he wasn't physically attracted to Jacopo, despite Jacopo's Nordic blue eyes and plush lips. He just wasn't his type—too fair, too thin, too gentle? Carlos, who was stockier and somehow more rugged, didn't have an answer for that—such was the mystery of pheromones and their chemistry—yet he knew he wanted to see more of Jacopo. He was smart, quiet, balanced, someone Carlos could trust and he could have fun with at the same time. Jacopo worked as an editor for a small but renowned publisher and also translated books from the French. Jacopo's life was busy, but not as frenzied as Carlos's, and Carlos liked the way Jacopo always managed to make him feel calmer, grounded, unlike the high-maintenance people he had to deal with every day at work. Their relationship had quickly switched from casual lovers to good friends, and the shift had come naturally, like an unspoken agreement, where apparently neither one was hurt.

Carlos persisted. "Do you know what I'm saying? About the pressure, I mean."

"I guess so. . . ." Jacopo was busy brushing specks of weed off the coffee table and just gave a nod.

"I think sex always turns the relationship into a power struggle," Carlos continued, his dark eyes flashing. "Maybe Clara's right: in a couple one of the two has to give up the ammunition and surrender. That never happens in a friendship."

"Yes . . ." Jacopo said, still concentrated on his weed-retrieving operation.

"I mean . . ." Carlos looked somewhere across the room, searching for the right words. "For instance, whenever I have this crazy fantasy of having my own child . . . well, the only person I can think of doing it with is you."

Jacopo stared at him with a stupefied expression.

"Don't freak out," Carlos said with a nervous laugh.

"I'm not freaking out."

"I mean, don't you think we would be good parents together?"

Jacopo quickly licked the rim of the rolling paper and paused, holding the joint in his left hand.

"Wait a minute: is this a serious conversation we're having?"

"Well, yes and no. I mean, theoretically, I'd rather raise a child with an old friend than with a new lover."

"What do you mean, 'theoretically'?"

Carlos shifted uneasily on the couch.

"With an old friend there's trust, familiarity, hardly any risk of splitting up. Of divorce, jealousy . . . all that stuff that happens with a lover. Plus the two of us would make great parents, I really think so."

Jacopo didn't say anything for a few seconds, unsure as to where this was going.

"I don't know, Carlos. I'm a bit—how can I say it?—*baffled* by this proposition."

"Hey, it's not a proposition, it's just a thought. Something I've been thinking about on my own and I thought I would share."

Jacopo looked at his watch.

"It's late. Too late to elaborate on this subject, I'm afraid."

Carlos smiled.

"Right. But don't discard the subject entirely. Think about it. See how it feels."

Jacopo walked home under a light drizzle. Although he had always been happy to be seen as Carlos's best friend, Jacopo was aware that their relationship was unbalanced. Throughout the years he had always been a quarter—okay, maybe half?—in love with Carlos. Little enough so that he could flirt and have sex with other partners and wouldn't feel too hurt whenever Carlos had a new boyfriend. Little enough so that he could bear the presence of an intruder between them.

That night, in his pristine white and gray bedroom, where no bright colors were admitted, he couldn't fall asleep. How long had Carlos been having that idea? he wondered. But now Carlos had planted a seed in his mind that had begun to sprout, and quickly became too big to get out of his head.

———

Because her affair with Gabriel was so new, Clara had been hesitant to discuss a summer plan with him. She didn't want to scare him away (what if by July he had become disillusioned or had already broken up with her?), so she came up with a strategy. She persuaded Carlos and Jacopo to share a house in Greece with her, and said she "might" ask Gabriel to come along. Would they mind? Of course not, they said; actually, they would be thrilled to meet him at last.

"This is the place I've rented for three weeks with a couple of friends," she said with studied nonchalance one night, as she showed the villa to Gabriel on her laptop screen. Only when Gabriel said he was surprised she'd never mentioned this plan to him did she ask whether he'd like to join them, as if the thought hadn't even crossed her mind. When he smiled and said he would be happy to, she felt victorious. The idea of having her best friends there reassured her. She wasn't ready yet to be completely alone with a man who made her feel so insecure, and moreover she knew that Gabriel wouldn't feel threatened by Carlos and Jacopo because they would do their best to make him feel welcome.

———

Carlos and Jacopo had insisted that Clara and Gabriel take the master bedroom, with its small, private patio and the view of the sea.

Clara watched Gabriel as he carefully unpacked his bag. On the plane and on the ferry he'd made polite conversation, but most of the time he'd been absorbed in his book. Yet he seemed more tired now that the two of them were alone, as if he had exhausted his reserve of energy.

"Which side of the bed do you prefer?" Clara asked him.

"You pick. I don't have a favorite one," he said without looking at her.

Clara sat on the left side and then lay back, as if testing the mattress.

"It's just the right firmness, at least for me," she said with a hopeful intonation. But Gabriel wasn't paying attention, busy as he was, piling his books on the night table on the opposite side. He had told her he was strongly opposed to e-readers and that's why his suitcase was so heavy: he was planning to read a lot. Apparently, his all-consuming job as a reporter at a financial newspaper didn't allow much time for reading novels. Clara glanced at the pile of books. It seemed more like a barrier or a wall that he was building on his side of the bed. But then again, she told herself, she should follow Carlos and Jacopo's advice and stop worrying.

This was the first time she and Gabriel would live as a couple under the same roof. In Rome, whenever they'd sleep together, usually at his place, they would part early in the morning because Gabriel had to be at the office by nine. There was just enough time to rush into the shower and then grab their cappuccinos and croissants at the counter in the café across the street. It was too early still in their relationship for Clara to feel comfortable enough to leave a change of clothes at his place, or ask him for the keys. What she observed now was that, instead of making her feel closer to him, their new proximity in Hera's house made her feel more estranged, as it heightened how little they still knew about each other.

Now she wished she could just lie down in her underwear and close her eyes. But Gabriel's presence made her too tense; she couldn't possibly fall asleep in front of him, just like that. She might snore, or breathe with her mouth half open in an unsightly manner. Daylight naps could look ungraceful somehow, unlike night sleep, which was more composed and aesthetically acceptable. She pulled her toiletry bag out of her suitcase and walked to the outdoor bathroom they had so admired, where an abundance of plants prospered in the damp air. The gray cement sink was surrounded by vigorous ferns. She pulled out her day cream, anti-aging serum, deodorant, feminine intimate wash and the drops to treat her toenail fungus and placed them on the wooden shelf at a safe distance from where Gabriel's shaving cream, toothpaste and razor formed a neat line. She put her brand-new electric toothbrush in a glass next to his and realized she'd bought one of the same make and color. Clara stood for a moment looking at the two identical toothbrushes facing each other inside the glass and wondered if that image had some hidden meaning. Then, as if on an impulse, she reached for the intimate feminine wash and the anti-fungal drops, and quickly returned them to the toiletries bag and zipped it closed.

Carlos and Jacopo had taken the smaller room, the one with the twin beds. They didn't care about the view or the space, as they didn't plan to be inside the bedroom much. They intended to spend long hours swimming and taking hikes in the evenings on the dirt trails that spiraled over on the hills behind the house. By now they had been on vacation together so often that they had become impeccable travel companions. Yet this time it was different. Something kept hovering above their heads whenever they were alone. The short conversation they had had after the dinner with Clara was still tormenting Jacopo. In the days that had passed since then, he'd felt more and more annoyed, as though Carlos had set in motion something that was impossible to ignore, and now he felt he was the one expected to break the silence.

———

One afternoon, while Clara and Gabriel were out food shopping, the two men were lying on a large daybed out in the courtyard under the shade of the giant oak, half dozing, with books open across their chests, when Jacopo, exasperated, blurted out, "Were you serious when you said you were considering having a child?"

Carlos immediately opened his eyes. "Yes."

"How serious?"

"Dead serious. I've been thinking about this for quite some time." Carlos was smiling, like someone who had finally gotten what he had been waiting for. But Jacopo was silent, his lightly tanned face held neutral.

Carlos prodded. "Have *you* had any thoughts regarding this?"

Jacopo needed to think before saying anything. He never thought he'd have this conversation with anybody, let alone Carlos. Had he ever considered becoming a father? No, simply because he never felt he had the right to. Sure, he often saw how he might end up being alone once he got older, and it was something to think about, maybe even worry about, but he always consoled himself by thinking that he'd be aging surrounded by a group of dear friends—gay men, mostly—and he would have Carlos, of course, who would be the closest. His childless, but close, loving family.

"Why me, though?" he said finally.

"I told you. Because you're my best friend, you're the most

responsible person I know, because you would make a great father and—well, because I love you."

Jacopo was aware that their relationship relied on a delicate balance, and he had learned how to maintain control over the ebb and flow of his feelings, never allowing jealousy to get in the way. So far he had succeeded.

But now, a child?

Carlos sat up, suddenly animated and energetic.

"We could have two, each with one of our DNA. Genetically they would be half-siblings. Although I believe that now it is even possible to have twins who carry both dads' DNA. I have to find out the details because I'm not sure how it works."

"Please don't rush," Jacopo pleaded. "Let's stop here—this is too overwhelming."

"Okay." Carlos sounded hurt. "Sorry, I didn't mean to upset you."

There was a brief silence. Carlos picked up his book and slowly flicked through the pages. The late-morning breeze was ruffling his hair, which was getting longer than usual. He looked healthy and strong, like a character from Greek mythology, Jacopo thought, letting out a sigh.

"I mean . . . you realize our lives would change completely? Actually, mine would, since you're the one who travels all the time for work, so I would end up being the one looking after them or"— he hesitated— "her or him . . . well, whatever they may be."

"Are you implying this is the reason I'm asking you?"

"You just said I'm the responsible one."

"You really believe I'd ask you to be my partner in this life adventure only because I need a . . . nanny? I can't believe you think I'm that manipulative."

"I didn't say you're manipulative. I'm just stating a fact. Maybe I'm not ready to change my life. Or maybe this isn't my wish."

"Okay, okay, I got it. I'm sorry I brought it up. I was impulsive. Let me just say, though, that whenever I fantasized about this, about a child, raising one, you were always in the picture."

"Which picture?"

"You and me and the children."

Jacopo hid his head between his slim hands in an attempt to cover up his impatience.

"Stop. Now."

Carlos figured he needed to lighten up the mood, and so he forced out a laugh.

"Okay. Just forget everything I said. I'm going to grab a beer—do you want one?" Carlos stood up and walked toward the kitchen door.

Jacopo assented and closed his eyes. He listened to the monotonous song of the crickets. Things could change so drastically at every corner. It was scary.

———

The first week in Hera's house proved a little difficult. The wind began to blow with an uncanny violence. It was the *meltemi,* Artemis said, the infamous northern wind that blew during the hot months. She came twice a week and made the house sparkle in no time, scrubbing the floors with an almost furious zeal. The wind could last for ten days in a row and drive people literally mad, she said. Carlos and Jacopo tried to ignore it and decided to go swimming anyway. But on the beach the sand kept lashing at their bare skin and got in their eyes while the sea was rough and murky with seaweed, and they gave up. There was too much wind to go for a hike or sit in the garden under the trees, so all four of them ended up staying indoors most of the time, reading, cooking, playing backgammon and getting tetchy when losing.

An underlying tension snaked through the rooms. The kitchen turned into a high-risk zone where petty resentments had to be contained. Carlos and Jacopo were early risers and they always laid the breakfast table for the other couple. They took care to go to the nearby bakery before eight, getting fresh bread and pastries for everyone along with the locally made yogurt, whereas Gabriel and Clara would eat much later with the indolence and languorous glances of people who had just had sex, and without fail they forgot to clear the table or wash their dishes. On the other hand, Clara kept buying delicious sweets made of pistachio nuts and honey in an expensive pastry shop up in the main town, and Carlos kept eating them in the middle of the night because of his insomnia. He never bothered to replenish them and Clara's irritation escalated, though she never said a word.

Every night, as soon as the wind quieted down, they were anxious to get out of the house, like prisoners at rec time. They made elaborate plans to try the different restaurants scattered around the island, comparing their finds on Trip-Advisor in the hope of being rewarded with amazing food. But somehow each choice turned out to be a disappointment: the restaurants were too expensive or too touristy, the moussaka and the fries too soaked in oil. They would drive back to the house in silence, each nursing resentment against the one who had suggested that particular venue.

The truth was that the new quartet was having a difficult time coalescing.

———

Gabriel was handsome and mysterious, just as Clara had described him: tall, with a dark complexion, a full baby mouth and straight chestnut hair that kept falling on his face on one side; he was constantly pulling it back behind his right ear. After meeting him for the first time, just before their departure from Rome, Carlos and Jacopo had discussed at length his good looks and specific parts of his body that they either approved of or were disappointed by, and they were thrilled by the prospect of spending three weeks in his company. But Gabriel turned out to be harder to befriend than they expected. He was gracious and well mannered, but often silent. His quiet demeanor intimidated them. They suspected it was a weapon he used in order to keep people at a distance.

"He's very shy, but he'll warm up to you; he just has to get to know you better," Clara had promised them. But his shyness felt like a barrier they inevitably crashed against whenever they attempted to endear themselves to him with their witty remarks, or get his attention by making smart comments about this or that. Now they could see why Clara was constantly tiptoeing her way around him. Whenever they made the effort to engage him in conversation even of the highest kind—discussing a novel, a movie or an exhibition they had particularly loved—Gabriel would listen to them quietly and then articulate in one sharp argument why he totally disagreed with them. They found themselves exhausted and disconcerted, as if all their efforts to make him feel welcome had only succeeded in making them look frivolous and incompetent.

Clara had brought along her watercolors and a special Japanese paper with the intention of painting, but she hadn't yet opened the bag where she kept them. She couldn't concentrate, or maybe she wasn't particularly inspired. Her head seemed to be always wandering elsewhere, mostly toward Gabriel, who could lie for hours in the hammock engrossed in a book, without paying much attention to what happened around him. She didn't exactly feel ignored, but she definitely felt there was a difference in the way they were aware of each other's presence in the room. She kept gauging every imperceptible reaction he had to her, every expression or shift in his mood. Each night, after they had sex, Clara felt they had made some progress, in that they had become a tiny bit closer than when they had arrived. But the minute they put their clothes back on, Gabriel seemed to retreat into himself again. What she really longed for was emotional intimacy, and that seemed so much more complicated to achieve than an orgasm.

————

They were coming back to the house from yet another gastronomic failure: a small tavern in a tiny village all the way on the opposite side of the island. Everybody was decidedly in a bad mood—sleepy, heavy with fried food and cheap wine. The car was silent, Gabriel at the wheel. He had somehow made clear, without actually saying anything—only by criticizing the way others parked or changed gears—that he was the best driver out of the three (Clara didn't have a driver's license; she had failed the driving test more than once and finally had given up), and Jacopo and Carlos had relinquished the driver's seat in order to avoid further friction. They actually found it rather amusing how, whenever in their company, heterosexual men invariably felt that the driver's seat belonged to them by birthright.

It was pitch-dark. The car, a four-wheel-drive Suzuki they had rented in the village, had been climbing up on a ridge and was now coasting on a gravelly road in the middle of nowhere, when, rounding a large bend, they made out a white shape in the distance.

"What is it?" Clara asked.

Gabriel slowed down. The fuzzy silhouette entered the luminous circle of their high beams. It was very small and looked woolly, undefined in its contours. As the car slowly rolled forward, the shape stopped and sat on its haunches facing them, like a tiny ghost emerging from the darkness.

"It's a lamb!" Clara said.

"Stop!" Jacopo said. "Let me go and look."

Carlos and Clara, who were sitting in the back seat, simultaneously started fiddling with the door handles, even before the car came to a halt. But the doors were locked from the driver's seat.

"Gabriel, stop the car! Let us out!" Carlos yelled.

Gabriel put his foot on the brake. He was the only one who didn't leave the car. With the engine still running and headlights on, he watched Carlos, Jacopo and Clara approach the thing. Leaning toward it, conferring. Carlos picked it up in his arms. From where he was, Gabriel couldn't make out what it was but he put the car in park and remained seated, as if to prove a point. Clara turned back, her face lit up by the high beams, and beckoned to him. Gabriel didn't budge, so she walked back toward the car and leaned into the open driver's window.

"Come see."

Gabriel didn't move. She touched his shoulder.

"Come on. You have to see this."

Reluctantly Gabriel turned the engine off, got out of the car, leaving the high beams on, and followed her. Up on top of the deserted ridge the night smelled of wild sage and thyme and the stars looked unusually bright. Down below, a deep ravine reached all the way to the sea. A black liquid mass, streaked by moonlight.

The shape they'd seen was a small fluffy creature with a thick coat of curly hair, and it did resemble a lamb. A small-size dog, perhaps just one or two years old, male. He stared at them with pleading honey-colored eyes, his soft head resting on Carlos's arm.

"Oh, he's so sweet!" Clara said. "What breed do you think he is?"

"I'm not sure. He could be one of those miniature poodles," Jacopo said.

"It's hard to tell what he is, probably a mixed breed, but he's too adorable," Carlos said, then he put the dog down and bent to scratch him behind the ears.

The dog didn't move, but again looked up at him with his big eyes, then he timidly wagged his tail and reached out to gently touch Carlos's shin with his paw.

"Oh, no! He wants you to pick him up again!" Clara said. "Is he hurt, maybe? Let's check if he has pain anywhere."

Carlos lifted the small dog again. Suddenly all four of them closed in, with Gabriel still slightly distant. They patted him along the spine, feeling his tiny body, checked his paws, his pink belly. He was frenetically licking their hands and wagging his tail.

"He looks in perfect health and pretty happy to me," Gabriel said.

"What's he doing in the middle of the road at night?" Carlos wondered.

Jacopo checked his watch.

"It's past midnight . . . a bit too late to let a dog out for a walk. He probably just got lost."

"Maybe he was abandoned?" Clara asked tentatively.

Carlos held the dog, brushing his muzzle with his fingertips.

"Yes, yes, don't worry, baby, we have you now, we're not going to abandon you."

Suddenly Gabriel intervened.

"We can't take him with us."

"Why not?" Carlos turned to him.

"This dog has an owner."

"How do you know? Look . . . he doesn't have a collar," Clara said.

"He's a house dog. Look how clean he is. And well fed."

Clara looked around. But for the high beams, there were no lights. Just crickets and blackness.

"There are no houses around here. I really think this dog was abandoned. I think we should take him with us," she said.

"Yes," Carlos immediately agreed.

"You can't really tell," Gabriel argued. "It's so dark we can't make out if there's a house anywhere near."

Carlos seemed annoyed by Gabriel's obstinance. He looked over at Jacopo, searching for support, but Jacopo just shrugged.

"I think Gabriel is right. He may belong to someone, and if we take him with us all the way to the house they'll never find him again," he said.

"Exactly. We'd be stealing their pet," Gabriel insisted.

The dog was looking at them with expectation, as if he knew they were debating his destiny. Carlos gave in and deposited him next to the low broom shrubs that lined the road.

"I think we're making a big mistake, but okay. As you say."

"Really? Are we leaving him here?" Clara asked, dumb-founded. "I can't believe we're doing this."

"Not in my name." Carlos glared at Gabriel and Jacopo, his hostility palpable.

They marched back to the car and Gabriel started the engine. As they carefully drove past the dog, who remained sitting and blinking on the side of road, Clara turned back and gave him a last look: she could hardly make him out, dimly lit as he was by the reddish taillights, but she could see his head tilted in what seemed amazement at being left alone so quickly by the very humans he had briefly deemed to be his saviors.

———

It was almost one in the morning when they reached the house. Despite the hour, nobody was sleepy or ready to call it a night. Carlos brought glasses, ice, tonic and vodka to the table on the patio where Clara was sitting across from Jacopo. Both of them were neurotically scrolling on their phones, pretending to be interested in their social media, so as to avoid talking to each other. Gabriel was, as usual, slightly separate from the others, wrapped up in the hammock just at the other end of the patio. A long, slim leg bent at an angle was all that was visible of him.

"Really? At this time?" Jacopo asked incredulously when Carlos placed the vodka on the table.

"Yes. I need a drink," Carlos said brusquely as he filled glasses for himself and Clara.

"I hate to think we left that little creature all alone up there." Clara mumbled. "It's so dark up on that hill. What if he gets run over? It's a miracle *we* didn't kill him."

Clara realized that she was annoyed with Gabriel, because of his bullish determination in leaving the dog behind. Disliking something about him for the first time felt almost liberating.

Jacopo poured himself a tiny shot of vodka, realizing Carlos wasn't going to do it for him. Clearly he and Clara had teamed up in some way against him because of the dog situation.

"Maybe what we should do is go back tomorrow morning and check whether he's still there," he offered.

"He may not be there tomorrow." Carlos threw a resentful glance toward the hammock. "The reasonable thing would have been to bring him here so he'd be safe for tonight, and then go tomorrow and ask around whether he belongs to someone. We made a shitty decision."

"I agree. Really shitty," Clara said gloomily.

Suddenly the hammock swayed briskly. Gabriel climbed out of it and walked over to the table.

He poured a shot right into the vodka bottle cap and swallowed it in one go.

"Okay, let's go get him."

"Really? You want to?" Clara asked, surprised.

"Yes, c'mon. If we hurry we might still find him just where we left him, or at least near there."

He picked up the car keys from the table.

"Who wants to come with me?"

Jacopo stood up.

"I'll come."

"Great. Carlos, you stay with Clara. And don't get too wasted."

Clara shot Gabriel a grateful look. She had never expected that he'd perform such a volte-face and turn out to be the one to take charge and fix the situation.

———

Almost an hour later Carlos and Clara had drunk nearly all the remaining vodka while waiting for the rescue team to return. Carlos had plunged into a melancholic mood after relating to Clara his stunted conversation with Jacopo.

"I'm not going to bring it up again. I'm afraid it was too much to ask. I scared him off."

"Why do you think?"

"He doesn't have a paternal instinct and . . . is that what it's called?"

"I guess so. And . . . ?"

"And he doesn't want to give up his freedom." Carlos raised both palms and looked away to show his frustration.

"Fuck freedom! Who cares about freedom?" she erupted. "Haven't we had enough of it already at this point in our lives?"

Clara gulped down a last sip.

"Anyway, you got it all wrong," she said, banging the glass on the table. "It's the other way around. Jacopo is in love with you; he always has been. The idea scares him because he's afraid he'll end up not just with all the responsibility and the work, but by being hurt by you."

"But why? Asking him to have a child with me means I want him to become a life partner of sorts—"

"No. It does not. You're asking him to be the father of your children, like a man asks his wife and then runs off philandering. If you're going to be serious parents you need to be a committed couple. I know Jacopo: he won't buy the idea of having children with you fucking around like there's no tomorrow. And guess what? I couldn't agree with him more."

Carlos looked at her, stunned.

"Really? But we haven't been lovers in ages and we—"

Clara waved a hand impatiently. She was drunk by now.

"Oh, please! If you want to have a family, then be a family, for Christ's sake! The least two people who want to raise a child can do is be in a relationship. Can't be a parent and have lovers right and left. You've got to commit, Carlos. The problem with you is that you always want to have your cake, eat it and lose weight on top of it."

"Wow," Carlos said after a micro-pause, retracting slightly in his seat, as if to avoid a blow. He was about to respond when suddenly bright headlights moved across the oak trees. They heard the car engine get closer, then it cut off, after which there was the bang of two doors.

Jacopo appeared on the driveway, Gabriel right behind him. Clara let go a sound, a mix of anger and disappointment.

"I knew it. Oh, shit! I so knew it!"

"What?" Carlos asked.

"They couldn't find him!"

Just then a little white furry ball shot out of the dark and came hurtling toward Carlos and Clara. It reached their ankles and ran in circles, jumping up and down, emitting short yelps. Everyone burst out laughing, exhilarated, while the dog kept shaking his tiny frame with excitement, licking their hands, sniffing them and running all around like a joy-crazed child.

"He was still there, waiting for us!" Gabriel said, his eyes glowing. He seemed more animated than he'd ever been before. "I don't think he'd moved an inch. I guess he knew we'd be coming back!"

"We put him in the car and he just rested on my lap, as if he knew me already. He just loves to be cuddled," Jacopo said.

Clara lifted her gaze just in time to see Gabriel hold Carlos in a brotherly embrace, then exchange an excited high-five with Jacopo. He then grabbed her by the waist and whispered in her ear.

"Are you happy now? You looked so sad when we left him behind, I couldn't bear it," he said, and kissed her on the lips.

Clara beamed: he had done it for her. He was aware of how she felt. So he did care, after all.

They gave the dog water and leftover chicken and, enthralled, watched him as he ate and drank and peed outside like a trained house dog. They prepared him a makeshift bed with a blanket they found in a closet. There was a short discussion as to where to place his bed, then it was decided it should be in the kitchen, at equal distance from their respective rooms.

———

Clara felt a particular ease as she was getting ready to get in bed next to Gabriel. He was staring at her with half a smile as she started taking off her clothes. She now felt comfortable and seductive doing that in front of him. It may have been the vodka, she thought, but something had shifted between her and Gabriel. For the first time she felt more in control, and he seemed more open, easier to connect with. She reached for the body lotion on the night table and started rubbing it on her hands.

"Thank you for doing that," she said. "You were so adamant we should leave the puppy up on that hill."

"Sometimes I tend to be too rational. But I have a heart too, you know."

"Of course you do," she said softly.

"Well, sometimes I give the opposite impression." Gabriel exhaled. "People think I'm coldhearted."

"I don't," Clara rushed to say. How hopeful, that he would confide something like that. She put away the lotion and lay on the bed next to him.

"If anything, I think you find it difficult to express your feelings," she said and leaned back on her pillow.

Gabriel didn't elaborate any further and remained silent. For a split second Clara regretted what she'd just said. Was that too much? Maybe she had been too direct. But then he pulled her closer to him and she saw he was smiling.

"I'm curious," he said. "I've been trying to picture you as a child. Were you some kind of tomboy?"

The idea that Gabriel actually had spent time wondering about what she was like as a little girl came as another surprise to Clara. She laughed.

"I was a pretty well-behaved child, actually, but I nurtured a vast trove of romantic fantasies."

"Such as?"

"Oh, I don't know. . . . I pictured myself living in faraway countries on my own. Sometimes I was in Indonesia living in a hut, barefoot, wearing a sarong, or I was a flaming redhead riding wild horses across the moors in Ireland. But of course I was never allowed to ride horses—my parents were afraid of everything. They wouldn't even let me swim if I had eaten a sandwich. They worried I could get a cramp and drown."

He smiled and curled his fingers around a lock of her hair.

"A redhead. That's so sweet. Nobody wants to become a redhead. Too many freckles."

Again he kissed her on the mouth.

They were just beginning to get closer, ready to make love, when they heard a sound outside the room. A light scratching.

They stopped.

"It's the dog!" Clara said.

Gabriel jumped out of bed, and as he opened the door the dog shot inside the room and hopped on their bed, frantically shaking with excitement, begging for more love.

————

They all woke up to a beautiful, crisp morning. The wind had finally quieted down, and birds were chirping in the trees. There was a new current of excitement at the breakfast table. Gabriel was in an unusually good mood. For the first time since they'd arrived, he offered to make scrambled eggs Irish-style and prepare a special smoothie for everyone. He pointed at the dog, who was happily jumping around as if he couldn't restrain his enthusiasm at seeing all of them reunited around the table.

"Guess what?" he said. "This little devil came to visit us last night."

"He slept curled up at our feet!" Clara added proudly.

The dog immediately sniffed and licked Carlos's and Jacopo's toes under the table, as if he wanted to show them he hadn't forgotten them.

"Doesn't look at all frightened, does he, or missing his owners, whoever they are," Carlos said, and the idea that the dog didn't miss his original home and seemed perfectly happy to be with them came as a sort of relief for everyone.

They decided to name the dog Hermes, not after the designer, Carlos specified, but after the messenger of the gods. After all, hadn't he manifested himself in a quasi-divine manner, materializing out of the darkness into the celestial light of their high beams?

Plans were made. They needed dog food, a leash and a bowl, and felt they should perhaps have him checked by a vet.

"Well, before we get all excited, we should ask around if anyone has lost him, shouldn't we? This dog is trained—he definitely belonged to someone," Gabriel said.

There was a moment of silence and for a split second it was as if a cloud had obscured the sun.

Clara looked at him expectantly before voicing her own assent.

"Well, I guess we should."

"Of course," Carlos said.

"I looked on Facebook last night," Jacopo said somewhat gravely. "This island has a page. It's mostly in Greek so I don't really understand what sort of things they discuss. But I guess we could post a picture of Hermes and say in English that we found him last night. This is a small island—someone is bound to know who he belongs to."

It was a good idea, everyone agreed, but Gabriel insisted, "I think we should make another attempt to find the dog's owner and go back where we found him."

"It was the middle of nowhere. There were no houses in sight," Jacopo objected.

"Let's check again in daylight, then at least we'll feel we've done all we could."

Reluctantly the others agreed, and they all got in the car. Gabriel was at the wheel, and Clara sat next to him holding Hermes, who, after two minutes, was sound asleep—the image of bliss. The car was silent. Soon after they left the house the road started climbing the ridge. After about twenty minutes, they reached the large curve where they had found Hermes, and they got out of the car. Gusts of wind carried the distant sound of goat bells. The landscape, seen in the bright midday sun, appeared barren and desolate, like a dusty desert. On their left was the top of the hill, dotted with sparse bushes and rocks, on the right, a steep path that descended toward the sea. A half-built structure that seemed abandoned stood on one side of the small cove.

"There's absolutely nobody around. I haven't seen a single house for the last ten kilometers," Carlo said.

Hermes slowly got out of the car, perplexed, and shot a worried glance at them.

"Shall we drive on and check if there's someone living farther up the road?" Jacopo said, picking up Hermes, stroking his fluffy coat.

A couple of kilometers ahead they drove by a small farmhouse. They saw an older woman bent in two in the midst of a vegetable garden, her head covered by a faded blue scarf. She didn't speak any English, and when she was shown Hermes she looked startled, then waved her hand, shaking her head forcefully as to indicate she didn't know him or want him.

They drove farther on, looking for another house, but there were none. They stopped to refuel still farther ahead, at a small gas station, and the young woman who filled their tank spoke good English. Hermes peered at her with curiosity from Clara's lap as the woman took a good look at him.

"Never seen this dog before," she said. "You know, here animals are often abandoned. Sometimes the children want to have a puppy but dog food is expensive, and some families can't afford it. So they take the dog far away from where they live and just leave them. It's sad."

They felt relieved and revived by this explanation, so the subject was quickly dropped. It was hot and they were dying to go for a swim, so they started to make plans for an excursion to a faraway beach. Jacopo volunteered to write up a description of the dog and post it on the island's Facebook page. Just in case.

———

In the following days Hermes came along everywhere they went. On the beach he didn't mind his new red leash and sat under the shade of a tree while they went swimming. He quickly learned how to wait outside a shop if dogs were not allowed. He seemed to have been trained to obey any rule in exchange for a bit of attention and was democratic in his preferences: at night he invariably left his makeshift bedding and randomly chose which bedroom to join, so that the two couples didn't compete but joked about the co-parenting scenario. Everywhere they went, people stopped to cuddle Hermes and children wanted to hold him; everyone agreed he was the sweetest dog they had ever seen. Each time someone stopped to fondle him, the four of them always made sure to tell how they had found him late at night on a deserted road, but nobody seemed to know whether the dog belonged to anyone. They also kept checking the Facebook page where Jacopo had posted a blurry photo, but nobody claimed him. As days went by and half the island was now aware of the existence of the lost puppy, they felt encouraged to treat Hermes as their own.

———

Carlos was tickling Hermes's pink belly, driving him crazy with pleasure. He had just woken up and the dog had immediately come to greet him with a lick on the nose. Jacopo was looking at the scene from his twin bed with half a smile.

"What are we going to do with him if nobody shows up?" Jacopo asked. "We can't leave him here, can we?"

"I'm not going to leave him here. I was thinking I should take him back to Rome with me."

"Really?"

"Of course."

"Are you sure? You travel so much, Carlos."

"He's a small dog. I could take him on the plane wherever I go."

"You don't know—he might grow into a giant."

"He won't. He's definitely a lapdog."

"Anyway, a dog needs to go out at least three times a day, and you're too busy at the office."

"Whatever. I'll find a way. I can hire a dog walker to do that."

Jacopo was pensive for a moment. Then he made a dismissive gesture with his hand.

"We don't need that. I can look after him when you're gone and I can take him to the park. It would be good for me. I need a reason to move more."

Carlos noticed the "we" and couldn't help but smile.

"Really? Would you be happy to take care of him every now and then?"

"Yes, of course. Actually, I'm a little jealous that he's going to be living with you."

"No need to be jealous. He can stay with you whenever you want. In any case, we live so close, it would be easy to share him."

"Exactly. We'll find a way," Jacopo said, and they both looked at each other, almost surprised, as if they had just made a big decision without even knowing it.

———

The vacation was coming to an end; in less than a week they would be taking the ferry back to Athens and then fly home from there.

The four of them were having dinner beneath a string of tiny lights in the *chora,* the quaint whitewashed village on top of the hill. Traditional sirtaki music was playing in the background and whiffs of fried calamari floated in the air. Hermes, as usual, was sprawled under the table, dozing. Gabriel and

Clara seemed more at ease with each other than when they had arrived, as though they had found a balance. She seemed less insecure around him and he was warmer, more present. Carlos and Jacopo had decided they had misjudged him at first, by thinking him pretentious and a snob: most likely he was probably intimidated by *them*. In fact, since Hermes's arrival, he had been much friendlier, as though the dog's rescue night had consolidated some kind of kinship among them.

Carlos made a swift move and announced he had decided to adopt Hermes. He had looked online, and there was no problem taking him back on the plane; he could travel in a carrier bag, and all that was needed were a few shots, which he could get from the local vet.

Clara remained silent. So did Gabriel. They were looking down, then they exchanged a meaningful glance.

"What?" Carlos asked.

"Nothing," Clara said.

"Come on. Speak up," Carlos urged her.

"Nothing, it's just that . . ."

"Yes?"

"I was also thinking I could, that's all."

Now it was Jacopo and Carlos's turn to look at each other with a certain apprehension.

"You travel all the time," Clara said. "Did you think about that?"

"Jacopo and I made a plan. It's going to be a sort of joint-custody thing. He'll take Hermes when I'm away."

"Oh. Okay, then," Clara said, in a disappointed, girlish tone.

Carlos glanced at Jacopo nervously, urging him to step in.

"We had no idea you would want to keep him," Jacopo said.

"You've never had a dog," Carlos added. "I mean, I never thought of you as an animal person."

"What do you mean?" Clara snapped back at him. "That's totally ridiculous. I was the one who didn't want to leave him behind, remember? And, by the way, what makes a person an animal person? Does one need to present a CV? I grew up with two cats and adored them, just so you know."

"Please, Clara, don't get upset. Nothing's set in stone here. We're just talking—no final decision has been made."

Clara dismissed Carlos with a flick of her hand.

"It's fine if you take him. I was just thinking that I work in my studio all day long and I spend so much time on my own, it would be so nice to have him around. I get quite lonely in there, you know."

Gabriel shot a glance at her, as though this statement had something to do with him. Instinctively he placed a hand on her knee.

"Clara, we could all take turns," Jacopo offered. "We see one another all the time anyway. Hermes can be our family dog. Right, Carlos?"

"Yes. Exactly. We should just continue with our shared custody. I don't see a problem. It's actually a great solution."

Clara relaxed, reassured.

"I like that idea," she said, and smiled.

They turned to Gabriel, who had remained quiet during the exchange, leaning back on his chair, slightly removed from the table. Was it too soon to consider him part of the family now? Nobody dared count him in yet.

Gabriel cleared his throat.

"That's it, then," he said, cutting it short, as if he needed to conceal his disappointment.

And that sounded like enough, at least for the time being.

———

Gabriel woke up with a start in the middle of the night. Something in a dream had disturbed him, but the image was already slipping away, leaving only its blurred shadow behind. Clara was fast asleep, and so was Hermes, at the end of the bed. He got up and walked outside. There was an almost-full moon up in the sky that illuminated the trees and the tall grass in a bluish silver wash. He sat outside on the day-bed and listened to the crickets and the sound of the sea in the distance. In a few days he would be back in the city, and he wondered whether Carlos and Jacopo would want to see him again, or had they been so friendly with him just because they had shared a house for a few weeks? He had noticed how Jacopo had referred to Hermes as the "family dog," leaving him out. Both Jacopo and Carlos had been so outgoing with him from the start, and he regretted not having reciprocated warmly enough. Gabriel also wondered whether his relationship with Clara had progressed in any way. She had been very careful not to push him, but he knew she wanted more, and how could he blame her? Why was he so afraid to let go completely? Why was it so hard to open up? It had hurt him to hear her say that she felt lonely. He thought of the extra room in his large apartment. Maybe, one day, she could use that as a studio?

A noise startled him—a faint, quick tapping on the flagstones. Hermes appeared. He sat on his haunches at the foot of the daybed, looking inquisitively at Gabriel, then hopped up next to him.

"Hey," Gabriel whispered, and kissed him lightly on the top of his head. He lay back on the bed, looking up at the moon that was peeking through the trees. Hermes scuttled next to him and placed his head on his belly. Gabriel felt the dog's warm body relax against his, and a few seconds later Hermes resumed a slow, regular breathing.

"Stay here, sweet thing," he heard himself say.

Gabriel rested his hand on Hermes's back, and pulled him closer. He wanted to make sure the dog didn't go away so that they'd sleep just exactly that close until the dawn came.

He'd never had a dog before.

———

The ferry to the mainland was leaving at nine in the morning. New guests were arriving the following day and Artemis, the housekeeper, showed up with a strongly built woman named Rhea, as extra help. Both of them were armed with brooms and buckets filled with cleaning supplies. They started stripping sheets and towels at great speed, and soon the house lost its familiar atmosphere. Clara, who was gulping down a cup of coffee standing up in the kitchen while Jacopo and Gabriel were piling their bags in the car, turned to Carlos.

"Isn't it strange, how quickly a stranger's house becomes your house? You immediately start calling it home, and then it turns back into an unknown place the minute you leave it to others."

Carlos wasn't in the mood for nostalgia, but he nodded. Gabriel and Jacopo walked into the kitchen and took a drink of water from the fridge.

"Car's packed—we're ready when you guys are."

Just then Rhea entered the kitchen and saw Hermes. She asked Carlos something in Greek that he couldn't understand. Rhea called Artemis, who was cleaning the bathroom, and spoke animatedly with her for what seemed a long time, pointing at the dog. Artemis was shaking her head, but Rhea insisted. She pulled out a cell phone from her jeans pocket.

"What's happening? What is she doing?" Carlos asked Artemis.

It wasn't easy to understand, but they got the gist of it. Apparently, Hermes belonged to Rhea's father or her older brother, it wasn't clear which, and his name was Whiskey. All four of them stood, frozen, while Rhea kept yelling into the phone to someone. The only word they understood, which she kept repeating was "Wheeskee."

The man was on his way, the women said.

There was nothing they could do, but mildly protest that they couldn't wait for much longer or might miss the boat. Rhea persisted.

"Two minutes," Artemis confirmed. "He come in two minutes. No problem for boat."

She was almost right. Eight minutes later, an old Fiat Panda stopped in the driveway. A man came out, wearing an undershirt, shorts and Crocs. He was covered in dust, as if he'd been working on a building site. He left the car running with the door open and, without acknowledging anybody, he walked straight toward Hermes, who was sitting next to Carlos with his ears pricked and a slightly alarmed expression. The man talked to the dog in brusque spurts, pointing toward the car.

Rhea nodded with approval when Hermes lowered his ears and slowly moved away from Carlos.

"What the fuck . . . ?" Jacopo let out under his breath.

Gabriel stepped in and faced the man with a stern posture. "Wait. Are you sure this is your dog?"

The man said something in Greek without even looking at him. He was clearly in a very bad mood.

Artemis translated.

"Yes, he say the dog always run away. Very bad dog."

Before anybody could say anything, the man shouted an order to Hermes, who sheepishly lowered his ears and climbed into the car without turning back.

And they were gone.

———

The four of them drove in silence to the harbor and dragged their bags to the ferry.

The way Hermes had been ripped away from them had been so sudden and so shocking that they had had no time to absorb the blow.

Finally, Clara spoke. "That man was horrible. Hermes didn't want to go back to him at all."

"I don't know," Jacopo said. "Maybe he did. Actually, I prefer to think that he was happy going back wherever."

"Happy?" Clara almost shouted. "No way. I watched Hermes. He was scared. I bet that man beats him. He called Hermes a bad dog. Hermes! And he just sounded so all-around nasty!"

"Stop it, Clara, please." Carlos was in a black mood. "Don't make things worse than they already are."

Gabriel remained shrouded in his silence, withdrawing further from the others.

———

The ship pulled out in no time. From the upper deck they watched the island get smaller and smaller and then, within a few minutes, turn into a dot and disappear. Its vanishing into nothing added another level of incredulity to what had just happened, as if everything that had taken place during the three weeks they had lived in Hera's house had become a mirage or a fantasy.

Whatever resolution the four of them had made or feeling they had welcomed and then nurtured was rapidly fading away. Their naïve plans of co-parenting, their silly fantasy of being a sort of family—all of that—felt almost embarrassing to them.

Once Carlos took a seat inside the ferry, his cell phone rang loudly. He began a lengthy conversation with his assistant in Rome about booking a hotel in London, where he was heading in a few days for Fashion Week. From there he was going to fly straight to Miami for the swimwear collections and would not be back in Rome until the middle of September. Jacopo glanced at Carlos: hunched over the phone, his voice a tad too loud, unaware of people sitting around him, already sucked back into his workaholic vortex. Somehow Jacopo had a feeling that Carlos wasn't going to mention the child plan again. It had been one of those scenarios that seem plausible in specific situations—a vacation on a Greek island was one—but then, once back to the practicalities of one's real life, inevitably fade. Jacopo surely wasn't going to bring it up again. Their life was good as it was, he reminded himself. There was no need for such a revolution. And yet, deep down, something was irking him. He realized part of him was disappointed, maybe even hurt.

Outside on deck, Gabriel was leaning on the railing, lost in his thoughts, impervious to the brackish wind. He realized he was looking forward to going back to his apartment and sleeping alone in his own bed. In an excess of optimism, only a few nights ago, he had been on the verge of asking Clara to move in with him. For a moment he had believed he was ready to take such a step, but thank God he hadn't asked her. What they had experienced during the vacation was only an artificial familiarity. Clara, Jacopo and Carlos were a triad and always would be; he realized he didn't have enough drive or desire to push his way into their circle. Seeing her twice or three times a week was the perfect measure for what they had—he was convinced of that now.

Clara came out on the deck and spotted Gabriel.

She moved in closer to him, her shoulder touching his. The back of her hand brushed his fingertips. He pretended not to notice and didn't take her hand. She waited for him to say something but he didn't.

"It's too windy out here," she said finally. "Would you like to sit inside with us? They serve very good coffee."

"I'm fine here. I prefer the fresh air."

Clara didn't move. Gabriel looked at her.

"Go inside if the wind bothers you. I'll come in a little while."

As soon as she moved away he pulled out his phone and resumed a Google search he had started the night before:

MINIATURE POODLES FOR SALE

INDIAN LAND

I was having dinner in a small pizzeria with Lorenzo, my husband, when my phone rang. The display showed an unknown number with a French area code. The restaurant was so noisy that I had to go out on the street to hear who was calling.

"*Bonsoir,* Sara, this is Daphne de Taillac," a French-accented voice said. "We never met but I guess you probably know who I am?"

The name meant nothing to me.

"Teo may have mentioned my name?"

"No. . . . What is this about?"

"I'm his girlfriend," she said and after a short pause she added, "I mean . . . we've been seeing each other for a couple of months and . . ."

Suddenly I felt a weakness in my legs.

"Has something happened to him?"

I had always feared one day I'd receive a call announcing some terrible news regarding Teo. He'd always been so reckless, prone to accidents because of his drinking, drug taking and mad behavior. It was a miracle he was still alive.

"Well, yes," Daphne said. "We were staying for the weekend in the countryside outside Paris, with people I work with. I'm an interior decorator. . . ."

There was a pause, as if she expected me to comment on this.

"And?" I said.

"Teo had a discussion, a completely absurd discussion with this cellist, an incredibly famous cellist, who, by the way, was the party's guest of honor, and Teo . . . well, he pulled out a Swiss Army knife and threatened to slit the guy's throat or something. We were asked to leave by my hosts—I mean, we were literally thrown out of the villa. We had to pack our bags and find a hotel somewhere in the middle of the night. It was scary. And extremely embarrassing, as you can imagine."

It was freezing out on the sidewalk. I took a long breath. I must stay calm, I thought.

"Where is Teo now? Can I talk to him?"

"At this point I'm not sure. On Monday we drove back to Paris in my car and he asked me to drop him at the airport. I left him at Charles de Gaulle."

There was a silence. I watched my breath turn into a white cloud.

"Sara? Can you hear me?"

"I hear you perfectly. I don't, however, understand why you're calling me and what it is you'd like me to do."

"I think he needs help. He was very distressed."

"Then why, may I ask, did you dump him at an airport if he was so distressed and needed help?"

Daphne pretended not to hear. Evidently she was in a

hurry to unload her guilt on someone else. Her voice went up a notch, anxious and more heavily accented.

"Listen, I hardly know him. We met only two months ago. He was incredibly charming, and then, from one moment to the next, he became unmanageable. He must have a bipolar disorder or whatever it is. He needs to be seriously medicated."

Her voice, through the crackle of a bad connection, sounded at once angry and accusatory. It was one of those moments when you feel like screaming no to whatever is coming at you one hundred miles an hour, when all you want is to go back to where you just were, which, in this case, was inside the warm restaurant, and continue the conversation with your nice husband about the movie you've just seen.

"I'm not his girlfriend anymore. He's not my responsibility," I said, but despite the determination in my voice, I felt a familiar crack opening up.

"I know, but he always refers to you as family. He told me you're like brother and sister. That's why I'm calling you. I promise you, he's really going to get in trouble if you leave him alone there."

"*There* where?"

"Wherever he's gone. Somewhere in New Mexico."

"Are you kidding me?"

"No. At least that's where he said he wanted to go. Please call him before he gets into more trouble. He needs your help, Sara. Now."

———

Teo and I had met in Kenya ten years before. He was half French and half Dutch. His family had lived all over the world when he was a child and he claimed he didn't really have a home anywhere. He was the son of a famous French aristocratic beauty and a diplomat, both professional socialites who didn't have much time for their children. Teo was handsome in a mysterious way, with his high forehead, white skin and fine bones, his sensitive hands and feet, and I fell in love with him in the space of twenty minutes, although we came from two very different worlds. At the time I was doing volunteer work in a veterinary clinic near Timau and lived on a minimal budget, whereas he was spending his family money pretending to be a wildlife photographer. In reality he got stoned a lot, drank and lived as though there were no tomorrow. I was envious of his lack of discipline because I had too much of it. I felt it restrained me and made me a boring person. I saw him as someone who took risks, who dared. His constant euphoria was contagious, yet I could tell there was an electric undercurrent to his moods. In fact, euphoria isn't fundamentally joy, but more like a thin veneer of hyped energy barely concealing a darker layer. I probably perceived right away that Teo came with a caveat, but like all people who have a tendency to fall headlong for someone, I decided to ignore it.

Now I also tried to ignore my exchange with Daphne, but then the thought of Teo wandering around the American Southwest, most probably in a manic state, wouldn't leave me alone. He had filled a big part of my life—we had lived together for five years in Kenya—and now, almost five years down the line, I was back in Italy, and I'd fallen in love with someone else and gotten married. Despite the fact that my feelings for him had mutated, Teo was right: I still cared deeply for him in the manner of a sister for an exasperating brother. All along we had kept in touch, and although I heard from him erratically, he was still very much my brother. So I caved in and called his number. He sounded excited. I knew exactly what that excitement meant; I'd been through it many times before.

"What's going on, Teo? Are you okay?"

"Hi, Sara—you have no idea how beautiful this place is, what kind of energy it has!" he chirped as though we had just spoken the day before, whereas we hadn't in months.

"Are you okay? I got a call from your new girlfriend."

"Who, Daphne? Don't listen to her—she's a neurotic and a complete nuisance. Guess what? I just bought a great car. I'm driving it right now."

I cringed. His rash purchases always signaled the onset of an episode.

"Why did you buy a car? Please don't start buying things."

"We need a car. It's a big place. Big country," he said.

"Seriously, Teo, you know you shouldn't spend when you get excited."

"I'm not 'excited.' I'm just in a good mood. The car is secondhand, anyway. I'm not that crazy."

"I know, but you sound agitated. I can tell from your—"

"Stop diagnosing me, Sara."

"Okay."

There was a pause. For a moment all I could hear through the phone was the sound of the car stereo playing what sounded like country music. Teo resumed his cheerful voice.

"You know what? I could move down here forever. It's a bit like Africa, same giant sky, same light. And you would love it. It's the perfect place for us."

"Teo, listen—"

"It's so great to hear your voice, Sara. I want you to come.

In fact you must—I should send you a ticket. I will do that, in fact."

I tried to explain I couldn't. There was work, deadlines, Lorenzo and so many other things I had to attend to.

But then I heard his voice break.

"Please just come. I need you to come. I'm serious." The tone had changed; it was pleading now.

"What is it, exactly? Try to explain."

There was silence again, only the muffled sound of a banjo.

"Teo? Please tell me. Is it like that time in Nairobi?"

Silence.

"Is it? Try to answer me. Please."

And then I heard that tremor again.

"I feel as if my brain is frying," he said.

————

The ticket arrived in my email the next day.

Rome/Atlanta/Albuquerque in Delta business class, which confirmed my alarm because it meant Teo was effectively on a spending spree, one of the many symptoms of a full-blown manic episode. I conferred with my husband, who was usually very understanding when it came to emergencies. He wasn't jealous, he said, but the whole idea of me going to rescue a manic-depressive ex-boyfriend sounded beyond unreasonable. Didn't Teo have any other close friends or family who could help? "You're not his nanny. He'll manage one way or another."

I was about to reply that there was nobody else who could do this—not the crazy mother, not the early-Alzheimer's father, certainly not the socialite antiquarian brother, who lived in Paris and wanted nothing to do with Teo's chaotic existence—when my phone rang. It was an American number. A man said he was a police officer calling from a station in a place whose name I didn't catch but was somewhere in northern New Mexico. The officer spoke with a Latino inflection, and said his name was Mendoza. He asked if I was a relative.

"No, I'm not. I'm just . . . um . . . a friend."

"Well, ma'am, you better call a relative. Someone needs to come and take care of Mr. Van Doorn. We've handed him over to the psychiatric ward in Taos. That's where you or someone else will need to go to find him."

———

Eight years earlier, whoever was around Teo when he had his first episode in Nairobi had dismissed him as drunk or high on some substance. At the time I was away, up in the north, treating a small herd of camels with a vaccine for MERS, a respiratory illness. By the time I got back to town, Teo's unruly behavior had escalated to the point that he'd been locked up in one of the city hospitals, nobody knew which one, exactly. I tried to call his family but they weren't very helpful. His older brother, Lawrence, put up any excuse for not coming to his rescue. He claimed that whatever state Teo was in must've been fueled by some drugs he'd taken and that he was sick and tired of getting him out of trouble. He also warned me not to alert his parents.

"They're old and unwell—they can't deal with any of this."

I finally managed to locate him at the Aga Khan University Hospital. Teo appeared in the ward's corridor, followed by a large procession of patients, all of them towing their own drips, like totems on wheels. They looked disoriented, as if hypnotized, like members of a subservient cult. Teo, the sole white patient, stood towering over them in a dirty camouflage jacket and a bandanna worn Rambo-style.

He looked insane.

"Good that you're here, Sara. I made friends with these guys. They're coming with me to southern Sudan," he announced. "Fuck wildlife—we're going to fight with the rebels."

———

Three days after Teo had called me in Rome, I woke up in the dark. My flight had landed in Albuquerque after midnight and I had taken a room in a motel next to the airport. It was only 4:30 a.m. I was heavily jet-lagged and knew there was no way I could go back to sleep. The duvet smelled of rancid polyester, and so did the mud-green carpet. I pulled the curtains apart and looked out on the parking lot: a thick flurry of snowflakes was dancing under a street lamp's orange light. The weather forecast for the day, printed on a sheet of paper on my night table, announced a snowstorm.

I had never been to this part of the world before, and was expecting New Mexico, by the sheer sound of its name, to be an arid desert populated by cacti. Luckily I had packed some warm clothes. I turned the TV on just in time to hear a woman announce that half of the state was snowbound and schools were closed because of the expected blizzard. She actually called it something else—a new term I had never heard before that included the word *vortex*. Great, I thought, just what I need. I checked the map on Google. I was supposed to drive 130 miles north in order to reach Taos. "It's going to be okay," I said out loud, as if by repeating the phrase, I could ensure that any obstacle I was bound to encounter on this trip would be removed by a mysterious force.

The car I had rented, the cheapest I could find, was a two-door vehicle without four-wheel drive. I had never driven in snow in my life, having lived for years on the equator and returned to Italy only a few years before. I asked the sleepy man at the Thrifty counter if it was going to be safe to drive in that kind of weather. Everything had turned white; visibility was next to nil. He didn't seem concerned about the blizzard that every news outlet was obsessively monitoring.

"You drive slowly," he said. "Just stay on the road with your lights on, and you'll be fine." I drove out of the parking lot into what looked like the interior of a refrigerator, holding my breath, guided by the soothing voice of Ms. Google Maps. This was the way I always approached any situation I had no control over: in a sort of blank state, without thinking, almost with my eyes closed, in the hope of dispelling the potential danger and making it to the other side without having to look.

Past Santa Fe, right after Española, the highway shrank into a single lane as it snaked down toward the Rio Grande. Then, all of a sudden, it stopped snowing and the sky cleared. It was as if God had peeled off a veil with two fingers; I found myself wading across an endless, luminous space. Taos Mountain, capped in snow, appeared in front of me, and on my left I could see the Rio Grande flowing through the red willows that lined the banks, its water shimmering with speckles of bright light. The road started to climb again. Past a sharp turn, I found myself on top of a high plateau; the mesa below me stretched all the way out to the horizon. A deep gash ran across its surface, slicing it like a knife cuts a cake: it was the Rio Grande Gorge I'd read about before leaving. I got out of the car and stood there in the freezing wind, breathing the resiny scent of desert sage and what I later learned were called piñon pines.

———

I managed to get Teo out of the hospital pretty quickly; they had no desire to keep him for much longer and, besides, there was no proper psychiatric ward as such in there, only a single neurologist. I used his credit card to pay an astronomical bill, since he had no insurance. I then had a chat with the doctor in her tiny office while Teo was waiting outside. He had to sign a form declaring I was his partner, in order for the neurologist to talk to me. She was a young woman with a mass of curly hair, wearing snakeskin cowboy boots and earrings made with feathers. The name on the tag said DR. CRYSTAL GOMEZ.

Dr. Gomez informed me that Teo had been lightly sedated with an antipsychotic, and she wrote down a prescription for his medication that he should take twice a day in increasing doses. She asked whether this was his first manic episode, and when I told her it had happened before, she said it was important that as soon as he got home he saw his doctor right away for further evaluation and treatment.

"You're aware that he needs to be on lithium for the rest of his life, right?"

"Yes, I know that."

"You should make sure he never stops taking his meds,

even between episodes. It's very important," the doctor added with a hint of reproach.

I didn't tell Dr. Gomez that Teo and I were actually no longer a couple, or that there was no one in his family who would come to rescue him. I didn't want her to think that he had nobody looking after him, that he was wandering alone with his madness from place to place. I also didn't tell her that when we had parted five years before, we had sworn that despite the fact that our relationship hadn't worked out, we would always look after each other. And I didn't tell her that, despite that promise, when at times I saw his name show up on my phone, I wouldn't pick up, because I needed to shield myself from what I still had a hard time calling his "illness."

———

But there was another problematic aspect of the current situation: Teo had gray eyes. Gray as in light-pewter gray. A color that did not exist in nature.

"What's with your eyes?" I said, when I finally managed to get him to sit with me in a coffee shop so that I could have a cappuccino and something to eat after the long drive from Albuquerque.

"They are new."

"I can see that. They make you look like a zombie."

He shrugged, annoyed.

"What are they? Tinted lenses?"

"Um . . . I think so."

"Can you please take them out? They scare me."

"No. They are my new eyes. You'll get used to them."

It was warm and cozy inside the café, thanks to an old-fashioned woodstove that burned thick logs. The heat fogged the windowpanes and the place smelled of wet wool and coffee beans. It was crowded with young people. Hippie girls in flowery dresses and heavy boots, men with dreadlocks or long hair done up in a bun were eating turmeric-corn muffins or gluten-free brownies with their soy lattes. Lots of Buddha and Ganesh images, ads for yoga classes, for meditation and astrological readings, were stuck on the bulletin board on the wall. The kids all seemed to know one another, and there was a lot of kissing and hugging going on anytime someone walked in from the cold. Unconditional love seemed to be the code word all around.

"I need to show you something amazing," Teo said. Whatever sedation Dr. Gomez had given him was already wearing off. He had that ebullience and breathless need to talk that I recognized as another bad sign.

"What is it?"

"I can't tell you right now. We're going to have the most incredible adventure, and I can't believe we're in it together."

"You should eat. You need to take your meds on a full stomach."

He waved a hand. His eyes were so light, almost white. They upset me.

"Can you see why we should move here?" he said. "Look at these people."

I looked at the hippie kids. They did look beautiful. But the use of the pronoun *we* worried me.

"Nice kids," I said. "What do you think they do here? Do they have real jobs or are they just hanging out?"

Teo shrugged; he wasn't interested in that.

"This land is innocent, it's spiritual. Can't you feel this vibe?

And this is nothing. I'm going to take you to a place nobody has ever seen. Just wait. It'll blow your mind."

———

In the parking lot of a restaurant called the Guadalajara Grill, we picked up the truck that Teo had bought only days earlier. An older guy was sitting across the parking lot outside a liquor store, smoking a cigarette in a drunken haze. I assumed this was the place where Teo had caused a major scene and the cops had taken him away, because the man, as soon as he saw us, yelled something in Spanish in our direction and gave a hoarse laugh. He must have recognized Teo, but I didn't ask for the details—I didn't want to know. Teo laughed back, walked over to him and patted him repeatedly on the shoulder. He kept calling him *amigo* but the man immediately stopped snickering and changed expression—his eyes had suddenly turned wild—so I grabbed Teo by the arm and pulled him toward the truck.

I dropped my car at the rental location in town, and sat next to Teo in his truck. I tried to persuade him to let me drive—Dr. Gomez had advised me it wasn't a good idea for him to be at the wheel—but he wouldn't let me. I insisted we go look for a place to spend the night, and opened Airbnb on my phone.

The landscape was stunning, the air crisp, invigorating. We drove right past a herd of bison with gigantic furry heads grazing in the pastures at the foot of the mountain. I wanted to take a photo with my phone, but Teo wouldn't stop.

"Don't act like a stupid tourist," he warned me.

"Why not? I've never seen a bison in real life."

He ignored me and kept driving.

"Taos Mountain is sacred, you know. That's all Indian land, Sara," he said, pointing at the thick woodland that covered the mountain, and as he did, the car swerved on the road.

"What exactly does that mean?"

"It means it belongs to Taos Pueblo and the tribe has lived on it uninterrupted for nearly one thousand years. It means its energy has been preserved. This is the oldest place in the whole of North America."

"Okay. Keep your eyes on the road, though."

"I'm perfectly in control of this car."

"Not sure about that," I whispered more to myself, and went back to my Airbnb search in an attempt to quell my frustration.

"Stop fiddling with the phone and listen to this—it's part of the reason why I came here."

"I'm listening."

"The Pueblo people were told by the Great Spirits to plant and harvest the land in order to survive, to treat their trees as their gods, to listen and to speak to them."

"Right."

All this mystical talk made me nervous, and so did the idea that there was a specific reason why he had chosen to come here.

"Basically, instead of controlling their land they believe they are a component of it. *A component.* Do you understand what that means?"

I wasn't exactly sure, but I nodded.

Teo started gesturing excitedly toward the mountain.

"Look! No clear-cutting, no buildings, no electricity. This land is still as God created it at the beginning of time!"

His careless driving was making me so anxious that I didn't want to look at the road, but I stopped scrolling through photos of comfortable-looking bed-and-breakfast rentals where I could finally get some sleep, and gazed out at the mountain again.

Its perfect shape, rising from the flat of the desert, resembled a giant *panna cotta* dessert fallen from the sky.

———

Downtown Taos was pretty in the way an artificial movie set is. Funky galleries and dusty shops that sold Zuni jewelry or cheap Native American art lined a street named after Kit Carson. Rich Texan tourists with brand-new Stetson hats took selfies in front of a hotel called the Historic Taos Inn. Everywhere I looked it was a feast of Virgins of Guadalupe, Frida Kahlo T-shirts, milagros and sacred tin hearts, discolored Tibetan flags flapping from tree branches and wreaths of bright-red chili peppers hanging on front doors.

Farther away from the center, the town took on a more authentic charm. Red adobe buildings were shaped in curves and smooth corners, carved poles holding the roofs of wooden porches. Scrawny mongrels barked in the back of rusty trucks parked on the side of the road. It was the West in all its glory, a scenery I knew only from a mix of old Westerns, Coen brothers' films and *Breaking Bad*. I began to feel elated.

Teo started to recite the names of the streets he had learned like a poem. They did sound quite evocative: Paseo del Norte, Camino de la Placita, Camino de la Finca, Callejon Road, La Morada Road, Penitente Road, Francisco Vigil Lane, Coyote Loop. We drove north, past the town, past horses in corrals, past clusters of aspen trees, then straight across the mesa. Way out, on the edge of the horizon, the Sangre de Cristo Mountains were blue, the color of distance. The sun had melted the snow in patches, revealing a deep-red soil. The sky seemed to press on us so closely, there was more of it than land. Teo was right: this was a landscape that called for joy—there was a clarity that laid everything bare—but I had no time to allow myself to be happy. This wasn't a recreational trip, or a discovery that could change my life.

"You need to take those meds," I said once more.

"I'm perfectly fine. I'm just happy you're here," Teo said, lighting a cigarette as he turned left into the setting sun.

He switched on the radio and raised the volume so he couldn't hear what I was going to say next.

———

The following morning I looked for Teo at the breakfast table of the guesthouse where we had crashed, but he was nowhere to be seen. The owner—an older woman in her sixties with long gray braids and dressed in violet thermal wear—made some remarks about one of the guests making terrible noise throughout the night, moving furniture, playing loud music, starting the car several times and probably smoking. I pretended not to have heard any of these disturbances and tried to divert the conversation by asking her about the house, a rambling adobe with thick beams on the ceiling and oval-shaped fireplaces that she told me were called kivas. She was a talker, proud of her past as a flowerchild who had come to Taos from Florida in search of a truer way of life. So I listened, patiently, although I was worried about Teo, not knowing where he was and what he might be up to after what had clearly been a turbulent night. The woman was in the midst of a story about the time when she lived in a commune and used to hang out with Dennis Hopper at the bar La Fonda, when I heard the truck come into the driveway and brake on the gravel. Teo walked in, still in the same clothes as the previous day, his eyes the same scary gray. Clearly he hadn't gone to sleep at all. He completely ignored our hostess.

"Ready, Sara? We've got to move. We have a lot to do."

I could feel his feverish energy, the way every fiber in his body vibrated and actually produced heat. His shirt was covered in sweat despite the cold, and he gave off a metallic smell. I needed to make him take his meds with some food. This was to be my task for the day.

"Have some of this delicious oatmeal," I said, making a motion toward the chair next to me.

He dismissed my gesture.

"Come on, we need to go."

I didn't ask where to; I knew there was no point. I just had to tag along until he'd come to the end of the manic ride and crash. Only then would I be able to come up with a sensible plan.

———

I remembered a time back in Kenya, only a few days after we had fallen in love so precipitously. We had gone to the coast and were wallowing on the reef at low tide in what felt like a tepid broth brimming with aquatic life. Tiny creatures were crawling around the rock pools while bright-green seaweed tickled our ankles and swayed in slow motion like mermaids' hair. Teo placed two fingers on my lips and gently pried my mouth open. He then leaned closer to me and, as I waited for him to kiss me, spat in my mouth. I drew back, shocked.

"What . . . ?"

He laughed.

"I just put a spell on you."

"How?"

"Now you won't be able to fall in love with anybody else but me. Apollo did that to Cassandra."

I laughed, delighted.

Years later, I checked the myth of Apollo and Cassandra and it turned out that Teo had it completely wrong. Apollo's spitting in her mouth was actually a curse he'd put on her, a terrible revenge after she had rejected him: Cassandra's prophecies were never again to be believed. At the time I loved the idea that Teo had somehow bound me to him with a lover's maleficence, using the power of an ancient god. I had no idea then that this latch between us would last this long, to the effect that even though our lives had gone in opposite directions, we still seemed unable to let go of each other. Maybe his action had worked its way in me as a curse, after all.

———

"Are those colored lenses you're wearing disposables?" I asked Teo once back in the car.

He ignored my question.

"How long have you been wearing them?"

He shrugged and looked away.

"I don't know."

"You can't sleep in them—it's not good for your eyes. I've

heard horror stories about people who wear lenses for too long."

"Stop talking about my eyes. It's fine. I like them like this."

"I just want your real eyes back."

He didn't answer and rolled down the window.

"It's hot in here."

"Please, I miss your old self."

"Stop saying that. I haven't changed. I'm always the same person."

Suddenly I felt something stealing my breath and choking me, as if I was about to break into tears.

"No, you're not." I said. "Come back."

———

We parked the car on the side of the Rio Grande Gorge Bridge, an enormous steel arch spanning the deep fissure that cut through the plateau. Teo looked down from the cantilever jutting out on the side of the bridge. The river was flowing at the bottom of the gorge like a silver ribbon, some six hundred feet below us.

We walked on the trail along the rim of the gorge. It was very quiet save for the sudden gusts of wind and the sound of our footsteps on the rocky terrain. The snow was mostly gone by now, the sun having melted most of it, and the air was redolent of dry rocks and wild sage. Teo was way ahead of me, restlessly jumping here and there, picking up pebbles and stones. I wasn't sure whether he was singing or talking to himself. After a while I caught up with him.

"Teo . . ."

He turned around with a jerk.

"Are you happy to be here?" he asked me, and then he added with an almost pleading tone, "I need you to be on my side."

"Teo, this is not about being on your side or against you. I'm just concerned about the—"

"It's incredibly important for me to be here with you. Because I know you understand this."

"What is 'this'?"

"Okay," he said, gathering momentum and making a sweeping gesture across the flat horizon, "millions of years ago, this was an ocean. We are walking on fossil shells, on what once was a reef. Can you believe that? This landlocked desert is a complete three-hundred-and-sixty-degree change from Kenya, and yet it is the same."

"I don't think I understand."

"What I'm saying is, this isn't a coincidence, as you can see. In a way you and I are back where we started out. From reef to reef."

He was exhausting me. I knew I wasn't going to last much longer.

I sat on a rock. "Please sit here. Let's just be silent for a moment. Okay?" I said.

He sat next to me. I could smell something mineral in his breath. He was quiet for about thirty seconds and then started again.

"Most people don't know that the coral reef is not a rock, not a plant, but a creature made up of millions of tiny living organisms that attach themselves to the skeletons of the dead ones. They grow, die and keep repeating the cycle over time. Basically the Great Barrier Reef is an animal about one and a half times the size of Britain. I should say it 'was' an animal, because it's dying. The reef in Kenya is dying as well—I went back to see it three years ago and I didn't recognize it: it's bleached and barren. No more coral, no fish, no algae. What's left is only the skeleton."

He stood up and stomped on the ground.

"This one, of course, died millions of years ago. But it was alive once."

Through his fractured discourse and agitation, I could see flashes of something coherent, urgent, even. Sparks of his old self came and went, like spurts of an intermittent bulb shining microseconds of light. It was painful to see it blink on and off.

I bent my head down.

"Teo . . . what exactly happened in France?"

"Nothing happened in France."

"I spoke to Daphne. She said you attacked someone with a knife."

He turned away and resumed walking ahead of me.

"Some asshole, not really worth talking about. And Daphne, yes, she can be charming, but she's too concerned about other people's approval. A fake artist, a fake recluse, always hurting and full of recriminations. You wouldn't like her much, I think."

"I want you to see a doctor when you go back."

"Not yet. Not now."

"You said you felt your brain was frying."

He pretended not to hear me, or maybe he was simply unable to concentrate on anything other than the frenzied energy zipping around his body.

He stopped and pointed toward the profile of the mountain.

"Look! Behind that ridge over there. See? That's the way to

Blue Lake. That's where I'm taking you tomorrow. There is a secret trail somewhere near the Pueblo."

"That looks really far to me."

"Not really. We can definitely make it. Anyway it's the reason why we came here. It's the place I told you about."

The landscape was lit with hues of orange and purple in the late-afternoon sun. I shivered.

"Don't worry about the trail—I've got a map," he said. "Someone gave it to me, but we're not supposed to tell anyone how to get there."

———

That evening we sat in a small restaurant housed in a two-hundred-year-old chapel, lit dimly by a few hanging chandeliers. The young waitresses looked like poets, with their rosy cheeks, wispy buns and long skirts. Even the menu was poetic: buttermilk yellow and blue cornbread, wild quail stuffed with green chili, home-baked tamales with Oaxacan-style mole, ruby trout wrapped in corn husks. The waitresses' heavy boots resonated loudly on the wooden floor, but the brisk sound of their footsteps was part of the western mystique and ambience: candles, a roaring fireplace, a tattooed cowboy shaking margaritas behind the bar.

Now that we were sitting down at last in a closed space, I decided the time had come to include my husband in the conversation.

"Lorenzo is an animation designer; he works for a large studio. They make incredible films," I started, but Teo didn't react.

"He's heard so much about you," I added. "I think you'd really like each other."

I wasn't sure this was actually true, but I needed Teo to acknowledge Lorenzo's existence somehow. Since I had arrived, Teo had never mentioned his name, or asked about him, as if the fact that I'd gotten married two years earlier were a detail he could ignore. Perhaps he couldn't cope with the fact that things had changed, and there were new people in my life who were close to me.

"I'd like you two to meet one day," I insisted.

He nodded absently, shifting in his seat, then made some gesture as to check his pocket for the pack of cigarettes and glanced toward the door.

"I need to have a smoke."

"Now?"

"Yes. I'll be right back."

As I waited for Teo to return to the table, I crumbled a pill into his tamale. He claimed he wasn't hungry, but I insisted he take a few bites. I kept my eyes on his plate to make sure he ingested the right morsel, like an assassin observing her innocent victim take the poison. It was exciting to watch him swallow it as he kept talking nonstop, knowing that the medicine would soon take over and hopefully rein him in. The next morning the crushed-up pills would go into his oatmeal.

———

Teo did have a map, a crumpled sheet of paper torn from a notepad with the circular stain of a coffee cup in its center. Someone had drawn it in precise maroon fountain-pen ink.

He showed it to me the following day, as we were sitting on the porch of The World Cup café with our takeout cappuccinos. More lovely hippie kids with long hair were stretching their sleepy limbs in the sun, sipping their caffeine next to a couple of well-behaved drunks. I read the tiny writing underneath the map: *The name of Blue Lake in Tewa language is Ma-wha-lo. Good luck,* it said in the flourishing handwriting.

"Why 'good luck'? I wonder," I said.

"You'll see."

"What exactly do you mean?"

He hadn't bathed in days and was smelling rank, of nicotine and sweat.

"This lake is so blue like no other blue in the world," he said. "A cobalt blue nobody has been allowed to see. And we'll be the first ones to see it."

———

We drove about ten miles north of Taos, then climbed quite a way past Arroyo Seco, toward a place called El Salto. The arrow on the handwritten map pointed toward a small trail where the road ended. The landscape was mountainous, snowy and darker. It was freezing, but the cold in my lungs felt clean and pure like crystal. We walked up the canyon in the shade of juniper trees and tall pines. The sun filtered through the branches, projecting blades of light on the snowy ground. A half-frozen stream gurgled in places. We had to cross it a few times, jumping from rock to rock. We proceeded in silence, listening to the snow crunch under our boots. As we kept climbing, the forest opened more and more till we reached a grove of aspen trees that still retained most of their yellow leaves. They fluttered in the wind, like tiny flags of shimmering gold. Teo stopped to look at them in silence. He brushed one of the tree trunks with his hand.

"These guys keep growing, even in the wintertime," he said as he scratched the white bark with his fingernails. "See this green layer underneath? It has some kind of sugary substance. It's food for elks, bears, moose, beavers. Aspen trees are like pastry shops for animals when there's nothing left to eat in the winter."

He looked up toward the canopy of heart-shaped yellow leaves quivering against the sky. I was hoping the meds would soon kick in.

"Aspens, like other trees, are genetically identical because their roots are all connected underground," he continued. "That's why they all change color at the same time. They even heal one another—did you know that? Trees send out alarms to one another when they are attacked by parasites and shoot nutrients through their roots to the ones that are withering or in danger. No tree is an individual. Think of this forest as a giant rhizome that shares the same immune system."

He looked around enthusiastically and shot his arms up in the air.

"Everything we perceive as separate is part of a single intelligence! The forests, the reefs, the shoals of fish that move in sync, the swarms of bees, the waves, the tides! Everything is connected. And the Pueblo people know this."

"I guess so," I said, even though I wasn't sure I believed it.

"I know you think this is a bunch of nonsense, but I've done my research. I know what I'm talking about."

It was true. The fragility of nature, conservation, destruction, climate change: these were the issues that had always obsessed him to the point of driving him into a state of anxiety and paranoia; these were also the reasons he had decided to live in Africa for a few years.

I began to wonder whether there might be some kind of design that connected the dots on a deeper level. Perhaps we were always meant to reunite at the foot of Taos Mountain. Otherwise why else was I here, following Teo, using a crumpled map drawn by a stranger, all the way to a sacred lake?

We moved forward and soon found ourselves back in the shadow of the forest. We hiked among silvery trunks, twigs, fallen branches. I had no idea which tree was what, but I listened to Teo naming them one by one.

Suddenly I recalled how, when we both lived in Kenya, we used to walk in the bush just like we were doing now. The two of us often camped out in the northern district, along the Ewaso Nyiro River. I remembered the red soil, the smell of dust, the thorny acacias, the bush ticking with insects and birds. We scanned, we smelled, we listened to the sounds of the bush, feeling the cool morning air brush our arms and legs. Every now and then we'd hear a branch snap, leaves rustle, something move quickly inside the thickness. There was always a moment of suspense, when I'd hold my breath, not knowing what would happen next, whether we'd come upon a buck, an elephant or perhaps a buffalo bursting out of the grass. At night we lay close to each other inside the tent, and if we were lucky, the distant grunt of a lion or of a leopard would lull us into sleep. When I'd awaken at the break of dawn, I'd find Teo, barefoot, with only a threadbare *kikoy* wrapped around his waist, leaning into the embers of the previous night's campfire, already intent on making coffee with the Italian moka he never left behind.

I had almost forgotten how good he had been at taking care of me, then. When he was well, before the manic episodes became severe.

In our twenties, at an age when one takes every miracle for granted, not only had we been in love, but we had shared an experience that was difficult to describe to others, to anyone who had lived only in a city. It was like sharing a secret we didn't need to mention to each other. We both knew we'd lived a life that was unique and unrepeatable—that was the bond that tied us to each other.

———

Now, instead of the African dust, I was inhaling the fragrant smell of chlorophyll and rot. There were droppings on the ground: I assumed it could be bears, elks, maybe. Dank logs covered in lichens and chartreuse moss were decaying and slowly turning into food for new, sprouting plants. Everything growing and dying and repeating the same cycle forever and ever.

I noticed that Teo was beginning to look tired, his features slackening, and something in his posture had started to collapse. The drugs were beginning to take effect at last.

"Shall we rest?" I asked.

"No, I'm okay."

I could tell he was struggling to keep up the pace. Suddenly I saw a dark shape flash through the thicket.

"What's that?"

Teo looked where I was pointing.

"I don't know."

"Could it be a bear?"

We stopped. Small branches cracked in the underbrush. A faint *clip-clop* seemed to be getting closer. Then the distinct sound of hooves clicking on rocks.

"What are you doing here?"

A man with a long braid looked down on us from a blond mare. His profile was similar to a raven's.

"Hey, man . . ." Teo started, waving a hand in what he meant to convey as a friendly, cheerful gesture. But the man pointed his finger at him.

"Where do you think you're going?"

I noticed he had a badge.

"This is Pueblo land and you're not supposed to be here. It's off-limits."

He pulled out a radio from his jacket.

A female voice came through the angry static and the man on the horse spoke to her briefly in his language.

"I'm escorting you down," he said, an icy inflection in his voice. "Move."

It turned out that the man on the horse was one of the wardens in the Pueblo Department of Natural Resources. We followed him all the way to the end of the trail, where we had left our truck. A car from the Taos Pueblo police was already waiting for us.

———

We sat in the blinding neon of Gary Salazar's office. Salazar was the tribal police chief, a gray-haired man in a blue uniform. He took a long look at the map Teo had been given. He turned it around a couple of times and remained silent. He then pushed the sheet of paper across his desk, toward Teo.

"This is a joke. Whoever drew this took you for a ride."

Teo didn't say anything and didn't pick up the paper. He was coming down fast, now. I could tell by the way he slumped in the chair, although one of his legs still quivered feverishly.

"Let me explain something you may not know, since you are not from here." Salazar spoke quietly, searching for each word with care, taking his time.

"Blue Lake is the most sacred of all our sites. Our creation story says that the Pueblo people emerged from its waters. Without it we couldn't exist as a tribe."

Salazar continued, tapping his fingertips on the table. "According to our religion, we'd simply vanish—you understand?"

I nodded, whereas Teo remained darkly silent, as if lost in himself.

"We go twice a year up to the lake to pray and perform our religious practices. These ceremonies are essential to the identity of our people. The presence of any outsider is a threat to the proper performance of our duties."

Salazar spoke calmly, though he was angry. Probably these were words he'd had to utter many times before.

By now Teo was leaning forward, elbows resting on knees, his face buried between his hands. Salazar paused, stared at him, waiting for some kind of response, which never came, so he turned to me. His face suddenly became more animated.

"That's why Indian land is off-limits to people outside our tribe. The Blue Lake area is specifically for use only by the members of the Taos Pueblo community. Your simply laying eyes on the lake is a contaminating factor that is life-threatening to us. What you two were about to do is a serious offense. It isn't just a matter of trespassing; it means breaching rules that have to do with the survival of our people."

I had zero knowledge of the Pueblo—a tribe whose name I had learned only forty-eight hours earlier. I felt ashamed of my ignorance: I had followed Teo in his quest, with his lunatic map, without having a clue of what we were doing and what codes we were violating in a place we didn't belong. The idea that laying our foreign eyes on Blue Lake might have put the whole tribe at risk of vanishing into nothing seemed at once remote and entirely possible. It was indeed a frightening thought.

"We are very sorry, sir," I said, forcing myself to look into Salazar's face. "We sincerely apologize. We had no idea there was a ban. There was no sign indicating we were trespassing and so we—"

Teo sprang up on his feet.

"I came prepared! I didn't have my real eyes!" he shouted, interrupting me. "These are not my real eyes, so I didn't contaminate your land. I knew what I was doing!"

Salazar looked at me, puzzled.

"I wasn't going to look at the lake with my real eyes!" Teo cried. "I'm not a fucking fool!"

He slammed his fist on the chief's desk, and a couple of officers immediately appeared to restrain him. There was a commotion for a few seconds. Salazar looked on, impassive. I wanted to believe he'd understood what Teo had been trying to say and that he had somewhat forgiven him. But I guess it was me imagining a better ending to the story.

The two officers took us next door and told us to sit down and wait. There was paperwork, forms to fill and sign, phone calls to be made. I was then asked to go get cash from the ATM machine across the street to pay our fine. I left Teo slumped on a plastic chair. He looked inconsolable.

As I was getting the money from the machine, my phone rang. It was Lorenzo. Since I had left Rome, I had managed to text him only quick and rather vague messages. He asked what was going on with Teo and when I was planning to fly back. I told him I didn't know yet; there were a few things I still needed to take care of. He said he didn't understand what else was keeping me there. Couldn't I put Teo on a plane, now that he was out of the hospital? Surely his family would make sure he'd see a doctor once he was back home, wherever that was. Once more he didn't sound jealous, only fretful, or maybe just hurt. I had a distinct feeling I was inhabiting two separate realms that didn't communicate, and for a moment it seemed impossible that I could transfer myself from one to the other just by getting on a plane. I was also completely unable to describe to my husband what was actually going on and where I was. I felt very strongly that the events of the last couple of days didn't make sense if put into words, especially on a long-distance call. I couldn't help but wonder how it was possible to be in love with someone who belonged to the other universe and therefore was unable to comprehend what was happening in the one I was seemingly stuck in. And why, I went on wondering, was I assuming—unfairly—that Lorenzo wouldn't comprehend? How come I didn't trust he would understand? How could we be close if I didn't trust he would?

I told him I was in the middle of something urgent and that I would explain later.

On the way back to our guesthouse, I sat in the driver's seat. Teo didn't protest and soon reclined his head and dozed off. I felt strangely peaceful: it was late, there was nobody on the road and, other than an almost-full moon, there was no light. The land looked beautiful bathed in that stillness. Suddenly I needed to pee, so I pulled over and took a few steps behind the car. The moonlight made the last patches of snow shimmer as if someone had flung tiny diamonds all around.

As I was about to crouch down, I perceived a sudden stir. A small herd of elk, perhaps six or seven, barged out from the trees on the opposite side of the road and ran across it, toward me. It lasted only an instant, but they came so close. Their antlers were black against the silvery light, like tree branches entwined. I held out my arm, as they streamed by and I felt the heat emanating from their massive bodies, their warm breath on my face, its pungent smell. An image of wild beauty packed with such power, bursting with life like an explosion.

Then they were gone again in a cloud of dust, of snorts and grunts, hooves clanking on the asphalt, back into the thick woodland, like a vision that came and went.

———

That evening at the guesthouse, I knocked on Teo's door. He was sitting on the edge of the bed. When he turned his face to me I saw that his pupils had returned to their original dark brown. They looked real now, but they were sad.

I pulled out the bottle of pills from my pocket and gave him some water.

"C'mon."

I sat next to him and I watched him swallow the pill. He looked smaller, as if his body no longer occupied the same amount of space as it had twenty-four hours earlier.

We were silent for a while.

"I don't like taking them," he said. Even his voice was smaller. "They make me feel like a Picasso painting."

"What do you mean?"

He made a vague gesture.

"You know . . . scattered all over the place. My nose here, my mouth there, my ears God knows where. Like I have no center."

I tried to laugh, but I too was feeling sad.

"But you must, darling. Promise me you'll keep taking them."

My job was over. I had succeeded in bridling the beast in Teo, at least for the time being. And yet as a result I had peeled a layer of protection from him, and now his pain was raw and too exposed.

———

I left his truck with the car dealer he'd bought it from and booked our return tickets. We would both fly to Atlanta, and from there he'd fly to Paris, where his brother lived, and I to Rome. I had called Lawrence's number from Teo's phone and told him he needed to come get his brother at the airport, that he was too fragile to be left by himself and that he needed to see a psychiatrist right away.

"It's a serious situation," I said, "He needs to be looked after. I've done all I could, but now someone from the family really needs to step in."

This time the tone of my voice must've been firm enough, because Lawrence acquiesced without any further comment.

We drove from Taos to Albuquerque and got to the airport at dawn. Teo slept through the flight. I had given him a sleeping pill because I was too scared he might have a panic attack onboard. When we reached Atlanta, I realized what a terrible plan I had made. An airport was the worst place ever for us to part: a capsule where people who were never supposed to meet collided only for the time of their transit and then bolted in different directions; a place where everyone's time was limited and where nobody belonged. One had to be very present in order to navigate this abstraction.

I walked him to his gate.

"Don't misplace your passport. Are you okay to sit by yourself? My flight is in thirty minutes."

I felt his hand grab my wrist. Suddenly he seemed as lost and intimidated as a ten-year-old.

"Are you going be okay?" I asked him.

He nodded.

"My head feels like a drop of ouzo in water. You know . . . cloudy."

"You're going to be fine. You can go back to sleep on the plane and Lawrence will be waiting for you at the airport."

His eyes still looked empty. They were two black holes. I'd been the one who had succeeded in killing whatever life they'd had, thanks to my tiny increments of poison. He was no longer manic, but now he was crushed. And now I knew I had done the wrong thing.

"I'll come see you in Paris, I promise. You'll be fine," I said, holding him tight.

I walked away and I didn't turn back. I just couldn't bear to see him hunched on that plastic chair, so small and scared, but they were already calling my flight.

Almost twelve hours later I was home, back into the other universe.

———

I had been away only a handful of days, but the time I'd spent in New Mexico seemed like weeks. I was frazzled, confused and overwrought. Lorenzo asked me about Teo, but I could tell he did so more out of obligation than real concern. I gave him a brief report, perceiving an undertone of impatience in his questions. He must've sensed that the trip to New Mexico had been a journey into my past, and I could tell he couldn't wait for us to move on with our life as a couple. He listed what was going to happen in the next few days: his brother's birthday party, a new exhibition at the modern-art museum he wanted to see, the Sunday farmers' market, and maybe a short trip to Tuscany, where he wanted to rent a house for the summer. I was jet-lagged and emotionally drained and wished I could just stay in bed for three days, but I told him I was happy to do every single thing he had planned.

I resumed my work in the veterinary clinic, where, instead of the injured wild animals of the past, I was now treating mostly cats and dogs that lived in city apartments. I didn't go to Paris as I had promised, but I kept in touch with Teo. I called him once or twice a week. He was still living in his brother's apartment in the Marais—an arrangement he didn't like very much, he said—and was once again seeing a psychiatrist. I could tell he was taking his pills because he sounded calm yet depressed, as if he had no spark, and he never had much to say.

Eventually our calls began to thin out; a month or so later Teo mentioned he had moved out of his brother's flat and had sublet a small apartment near Place de la Bastille. He was planning to stay there for a while, and he was seeing Daphne again, on and off. A friend of his, a photo editor for an online art and culture magazine, had offered to give him some work as a photographer. Teo still sounded joyless, but at least I felt that he was beginning to resurface. I called him again a few times but he never answered and didn't return my calls.

I thought it was a good sign.

———

It was spring. Early one morning I was at the clinic dealing with a feisty Siberian cat that needed a shot and was giving me a hard time. Lorenzo called once, twice. I didn't pick up the phone until I was done and my client had left. Then I called him back.

"I wanted you to hear it from me before you read it in the paper. It's about Teo."

"What happened?"

Once again my knees gave way. So this was it—the call I'd always feared. Lorenzo had just seen the headline on the *La Repubblica* website: WILDLIFE PHOTOGRAPHER SUICIDE IN PARIS. Teo had jumped off a bridge into the Seine, a few blocks from his brother's apartment.

"I'm so sorry," he said. "I know how close you two were. Please come home. I won't be going to the studio; I'll be here if you need me."

I was devastated and I was angry too, as one always is when someone leaves us like that, without warning, without even asking for help.

So many questions I had no answers to haunted me for a long time. Why? Had he stopped taking the meds? Was that the reason he had plunged into such a hopeless depression? Why had I not tried harder when he had stopped answering my calls? Was it because I wanted to believe he was feeling better so I could stop worrying about him and live my life in peace? It seemed so cruel that his only options were reduced to manic euphoria or deepest gloom. But bipolar disorder meant exactly that: it was either North Pole or South Pole, with nothing in between. He must've been exhausted living like this, like a pendulum constantly swinging from one excess to the other.

With time our last encounter in Taos acquired a sort of magical tint, a strange adventure that to me now, years later, seems more like a dream: Teo's new eyes; our mission to Blue Lake, whose color white people were not supposed to see; a fake map written on a crumpled piece of paper; the forest and the aspen trees that connected their roots underground and changed their color simultaneously.

But most of all it was the elks' apparition in the moonlight that stayed with me. In the following years I always connected that flash of wildness to Teo, like a reminder that those parallel lives of secret and mostly invisible creatures living in northern forests or the dense African bush had always been around us, closer than we imagined, and always would be. The thought reassured me, as if the glimpse I had caught of them had been a message from him to me and me only.

THERE MIGHT BE BLOOD

Diana told her friends she was going to take some time off from her marriage, making it sound like a whimsical plan. She called it "an adventure of self-discovery," smirking in a self-deprecating way to show it was meant ironically. The plan included a novel—*the* novel she claimed she had always meant to write—in case anybody wondered what she was going to do for two months in Rome by herself. Friends encouraged her—how could they not?—but most of them figured there must be serious trouble between her and Mark. Nobody knew exactly what—they had always been very private, careful to project the image of a solid couple. To her friends Diana didn't seem the type of woman who suddenly needed her independence so badly as to leave her husband in New York and move to a city where she didn't know anybody and didn't speak the language. The idea that she was going to write a novel also sounded ludicrous, even pitiable.

Mark seemed indifferent to Diana's preparations for her journey. Throughout their relationship, even before their marriage, he had always been the one calling the shots, and now, for the first time, he found himself waiting for her next move. At first he thought her idea to live in Rome for two months was just a tactic to punish him and didn't believe she would go through with it. Only when she announced she had canceled, until her return, all the classes at Diana's Kitchenworks— the successful cooking school she had opened a few years earlier—did he realize she was actually leaving him, although temporarily. He didn't ask questions but he sulked, in the passive-aggressive way that lately had become a familiar trait of his.

Diana had found a sublet on a website called Rome for Nomads, a fitting name for those who despised the idea of being just a tourist. The site listed "a trove of secret information for the experienced traveler" and, in addition to authentic restaurants and great shopping tips, it advertised charming places to stay and feel at home "and live the way Romans do." The apartment she picked was near Piazza Navona, right in the heart of the city. A top floor with a terrace in a palazzo built in the seventeenth century that bore the name of the ancient family—princes, it appeared—whose descendants still occupied one entire floor. It was expensive, but she had done some clever haggling with the owner, and because it was going to be a long-term sublet, she managed to get a considerable discount.

She had been to Rome before, way back, with two girl-friends from college. At the time they were backpacking, living on thirty dollars a day, and they slept in one room in some shabby pensione by the train station. She remembered only fragments of that trip: the chaotic traffic, the exhausting walks through the Colosseum and the Vatican museums, one heavenly carbonara, making out with a pretty Italian boy who sold them hashish in Piazza di San Calisto.

Diana felt shaky and fragile during the weeks that preceded her departure. Being separated from Mark for that long seemed but a rehearsal for what her future life could turn out to be.

And once she took her seat on the plane, she knew there was no going back: what she had methodically planned and cheerfully talked about to friends was no longer a fantasy. She took a sleeping pill and drank a glass of cheap spumante to dull her nerves. Had she been too impulsive? Was this separation really necessary? She leaned back on the polyester adjustable headrest and sighed. Well, it was too late to find out.

A month earlier, on a cold evening in Brooklyn, Diana had been in tears, walking home beside Mark from the subway.

As they turned a corner from Lafayette, they saw the girl coming toward them. She looked glamorous and fresh on her bicycle, with an old felt hat and long, bare legs showing from under her black coat. She worked in an expensive vintage clothing shop right in their neighborhood, so it wasn't such an extraordinary coincidence that she should appear just as they were talking about her. The strange thing was that Diana never used to run into her before, whereas now the girl seemed to pop up on every corner. Maybe Diana had never paid attention—and why would she?—but now she wished she could un-know her face. The girl was pedaling toward them with a lopsided smile, as if conceived at the very last minute because of the speed of their unexpected clashing into each other. Her tentative smile could have meant two different things: seeing Mark and deciding to acknowledge him at the very last moment in order to keep up appearances and retain her dignity, or maybe—more possible—her expression wasn't a smile at all, but a grin meant to show them her contempt. Diana cringed. Here they were, the older wife trying to pick up the pieces of their marriage after the girl had fucked her husband.

The girl disappeared in a flash of pale hair and white skin. There was a moment of tense silence.

"That was your friend."

Mark pretended not to hear.

"Wasn't it?" she insisted.

Mark didn't say anything.

"With bare legs, pretending not to be cold in February."

He shrugged and turned his head away from her.

"Of course it was!" Diana wiped what was left of a tear with her gloved hand.

"Please. Let's not ruin the day by continuing this conversation," he muttered, as he quickened his pace.

That night Diana had a dream in which Mark was confessing some other infidelity. The dream had produced a vivid rage, as real as her reaction when Mark had first admitted the affair. Despite the revelations, the tears, the promises and the impromptu, desperate sex they'd had in the wake of his confession, the dream was a warning: it told her that her fury was still intact, latent, only waiting to explode again. No, she just couldn't forgive him.

As soon as Diana stepped through the grand entrance of the ancient palazzo she smelled a mix of marble and moss. It was early morning, and the inner courtyard was still quiet: a cluster of orange trees gave off a fresh whiff of citrus and a fountain covered in maidenhair fern dribbled into a large shell-shaped basin. The *portiere* was a small man with a patch of sparse hair, wearing a worn-out uniform with a couple of loose buttons dangling from the jacket. He introduced himself as Massimo in heavily accented English and took her luggage.

"I'm sorry, *signora,* but they didn't have elevators four hundred years ago. We'll have to walk up to the fifth floor," he said, leading her toward the large spiral staircase.

"No problem at all!" she replied cheerfully. She certainly wasn't going to complain about living in a seventeenth-century palazzo. "Four hundred years? That's just wonderful!"

The stairs resembled a giant nautilus shell. Massimo noticed her awe.

"The palace was designed by Borromini," he said proudly. "The staircase is a masterpiece. It's in Wikipedia."

Diana followed him slowly, savoring each step, stopping on each landing to admire the big wooden doors, the tall, vaulted ceilings. On the fourth floor she stopped to catch her breath while Massimo kept on going. Then the staircase shrank, as did the doors. Servants' quarters, Diana thought, given the more human proportions. At the top of the very last flight of stairs, which were steeper and more reasonably sized, Massimo was waiting for her with her suitcases, in front of an open door. She walked in.

She wanted to scream with joy. A slanting ceiling, thick ancient beams, tons of light. Old kilims covered the diamond-shaped tiles, Afghan textiles draped the sofas. There were lots of books on the shelves, old paintings on the walls and a perfectly equipped kitchen. The three rooms were like train compartments—one ran into the next in a straight line, and once all the doors were opened, one could look all the way through to the end. Massimo brought in the two heavy suitcases and stood next to her by the large window as she was taking in the view of roofs that stretched below her. Oval cupolas and bell towers dotted the red terra-cotta landscape. She opened the door to the terrace and walked out.

"Don't go out, please, *signora!*" Massimo pointed toward a chimney that sprouted on the slanting tiles. "No, no, please! There's a family of seagulls right in there. It's better you remain inside. These gulls can become very aggressive. One of them attacked the guest who was staying here just before you. And now they are nesting."

"How dangerous can seagulls be?" Diana asked.

"They are big birds, and they can badly hurt you, *signora.* We had to take that gentleman to the hospital to get stitches on his head. The landlord recommended you stay indoors."

Diana retreated inside. How inconvenient. She wanted to use the terrace—after all, she had paid for it. How much longer would it take for the seagulls to hatch the eggs? she asked Massimo. And wasn't there a way to get rid of them?

Massimo opened his arms and looked up at the sky as if forwarding her questions to heaven.

———

Her first few days in Rome were exciting. Everything she did made her unreasonably happy: she picked the first *carciofi romaneschi* in Campo dei Fiori, found a beautiful old porcelain plate at the Porta Portese flea market, discovered a small Cara-vaggio in the way back of a dark church, bought a Borsalino hat. There was joy to all her finds, a sense of vibrancy.

The therapist she and Mark had been seeing had insisted that in order to reinstate trust they should speak daily dur-ing this separation (Mark had admitted he had no excuses for cheating on her and had sworn he would never see that young girl again). Apparently, frequent communication played a crucial part in the healing process.

Diana called her husband daily and related to him what she had done during the day. He listened, but he was uninter-ested; she could tell by his voice. None of the things that were making her happy grabbed his attention. On the contrary, he withstood her descriptions as if listening to her adventures was simply one of the many penalties he had to pay out for his infidelity. When his turn came to recount his day, it was always a new ache, a new interesting pain, described in a very elaborate way: one day it was a cramp like an octopus clutch-ing his lower abdomen, another day it was air being sucked out of his lungs by a strange force. All his symptoms sounded terrifying but didn't lead to any identifiable condition. The conversations rekindled her anger, which then took a few hours to disperse.

Several days after her arrival, she told him she had finally started to write.

"I began something last night," she said. "I feel I'm coming back into my old self."

She wanted him to believe in her project but, more impor-tant, she longed for him to see her in a different light, awash in the same glow as when they had first fallen in love. Soon after they'd met she had shown him some of her poetry (while she was still in college, a small collection of her poems was published by a small press) and Mark had praised it with enthusiasm and encouraged her to continue. A couple of years later, right after they were married, she had flown across the country for a writing workshop in Portland, where she had produced a couple of short stories. Mark read them, this time with less enthusiasm, she felt. He made a few comments (some clichés, a couple of unrealistic twists) and Diana had perceived a new condescending tone that irritated her. After all, Mark was an architect and hardly ever read fiction. What made him such an expert? Yet his lukewarm reaction had made her feel more insecure. After receiving Mark's comments she decided it was best to keep her writing for herself. One day at breakfast she announced she had been taking notes for a novel.

"That's great," Mark said, pouring himself more coffee. "I'm happy to read something whenever you are ready."

In the months that followed, he avoided asking about her literary progress and she never mentioned it to him. Meanwhile Diana had started teaching cooking classes here and there, an activity she considered only temporary and not a career. But her classes became an overnight success and soon she rented a space in Fort Greene and turned it into a proper school. Diana's Kitchenworks got written up in the *New York Times* food section and the Brooklyn food blogs, while the little red notebook filled with her scribbles ended up in a drawer. Now that same notebook, revived after its long sleep, lay on her desk in Rome.

Unfortunately what she had told Mark on the phone that day wasn't exactly true. She had spent hours reading the notebook's contents, which she had almost forgotten, and to her surprise she found the writing naïve, almost embarrassing. So far she'd written only a couple of paragraphs, edited them laboriously, reread them the night before and lost interest in what she had accomplished. The words sounded pretentious and sentimental and the story outdated. Diana felt humiliated by this false start and decided to give herself another few days before opening the notebook again. She was beginning to wonder whether the actual goal of her move to Rome was to find her voice as a writer. Did she really have a novel in her, as the writing-workshop cliché always went? Or was she simply training herself to be Diana minus Mark, and find out what was left of her without him and Diana's Kitchenworks? Who was this "old self" she was claiming to have found again? All these questions troubled her. She hadn't searched for real answers in so long, and feared it might be dangerous to dig too deeply at a time when she felt so kaleidoscopically vulnerable.

––––––

It had been raining on and off since she had arrived. *Marzo pazzo,* March madness, Massimo called it. Whenever she came into or out of the palazzo, she enjoyed their quick exchange in her stilted Italian and his stilted English. She noticed, though, that whenever she spoke to Massimo, to the vendors in the market or to the barista from whom she ordered her espresso, she always used a hesitant tone. It wasn't just the language. She wasn't sure about anything here. Why did people ask for cappuccino *al vetro* and drink it in a small glass? How was one supposed to eat those weird spindly greens, curled like a cork opener, called *puntarelle*? Where did one actually buy a ticket for the bus if not on the bus itself? Being a visitor had a humbling effect; one was stripped of any authority and pushed back into childhood again.

She decided to do something useful and spend a day around the Forum with a guidebook. She had seen a magazine post about a newly excavated Roman villa adjacent to the Trajan column, which had just been opened to visitors. The house, the article said, was perfectly preserved and the mosaics and frescoes were stunning. At least, Diana thought, she'd be surrounded by other people like her, helpless tourists who had no answers to their many questions and spoke like children to baristas. But the day was gray and drizzly, and the Forum dampened her mood. Diana and a large group were led down a staircase, deep down in what the guide dramatically described as "the bowels of Imperial Rome." The interior of what was left of the villa was dark and chilly. There was so much stuff buried beneath the pavement, Diana thought—layers and layers of history. Most of Rome was invisible, inexplicable. The ruins depressed her, as did the freezing underground rooms of the villa. Maybe Rome was a metaphor for the subconscious: its contents were buried in deep chambers of history whose fragments floated to the surface so randomly that the effect was destabilizing.

After a week or so, her daily routines—the morning run along the riverbanks, the fussy, intricate food shopping, her meticulously cooked meals—became empty rituals. Now that she was taking a pause from writing, the days felt endless. Instead of revealing something new, the long hours made her feel lonely, isolated and, if anything, silly.

She spent too much time indoors because of the rain. The light that filled the rooms was livid, the apartment too quiet.

Familiar objects sat still in their places as if they had no purpose. She had fallen into a vacuum, or maybe to the bottom of the sea.

———

But toward the end of March, Diana woke up one day to find the apartment bathed in a new, stark, beautiful light. She opened the windows to let the sun warm her skin. The air was sweeter and carried a new fragrance. Ignoring Massimo's warning, Diana decided to take her cup of coffee outside. She stepped out in her bare feet, enjoying the warmth of the terracotta tiles under her soles. Her mood shifted immediately: she noticed new juicy buds on the bare branches of the hydrangeas, the first daffodils were beginning to sprout and sparrows were chirping.

She sat in the sun with her eyes closed, breathing slowly, trying to savor that moment of bliss. Maybe all she'd needed was a little time to reorient. After all, being on her own, without having to work, was a new state of mind. That's when she heard a low, insistent sound coming closer to her. Diana opened her eyes just in time to see a white streak, giant wings flapping low over her head. She ducked to avoid the strike of the bird's razor-sharp claws. She ran inside and frantically shut the French door. The seagull kept wailing, and its racket alerted three more birds, which came flying from different directions, ready to fight the enemy as a team. The wailing seagull was the biggest of them all, with wings that spanned almost five feet. Diana and the bird were face-to-face. She met its glaucous red-circled eyes; filled with rage; the bird thumped its beak repeatedly on the glass. At such close range, it looked wilder and dirtier than the ones she had seen darting across the river during her morning runs; some of its feathers were broken and stained by soot. They stared at each other with hatred. She felt as if her future assassin had singled her out and wasn't going to forget what she looked like.

———————

"I say, please no go on terrace, *signora!*" Massimo held out his hands and looked up to the heavens above, exasperated. There was nothing they could do, he said in his halting English. He and the handyman who worked around the palazzo had tried everything to keep the seagulls away: alarms, ultrasonic devices, a reflective scare tape, scarecrows in the shape of owls. Nothing worked. One just had to be patient and wait for the hatching season to come to an end.

"Nonsense. There must be a way to get rid of them!" Diana snapped, and realized she was using her old grown-up voice at last.

Seagulls are monogamous creatures that mate for life and rarely divorce. They have a strong societal structure that works effectively against predators to their breeding colonies, as they will gang up on the intruder with up to a hundred gulls and drive them away.

Diana stared at the page she'd just Googled. She added the word ROME to SEAGULL ATTACK, and a new list of articles popped up. Apparently, the birds' numbers had been rising since the first couple mated on the terrace of a famous ethologist back in 1971. Tens of thousands had been counted years back, but by now even that number might have more than doubled; it was impossible to keep track of them. Children had been targeted by hungry gulls, sandwiches seized from their hands; old ladies had been taken to emergency rooms with bleeding heads; the population of house sparrows had been decimated; a Chihuaha had been dismembered and left half eaten. Tourists were no longer allowed to have breakfast on the terraces of their quaint hotels because of the ferocious gangs of avian families. The seagulls "had become an army of barbaric invaders," one page declared. Fueled by the adrenaline produced by her encounter, Diana tweaked her search, typing two words into the Google home page: SEAGULL REMOVAL.

———

The man's name was Ivo.

He sounded quiet and professional on the phone. His English was flawless—apparently, he'd spent a few years in Canada working on a farm. He listened to Diana recounting the attack on the roof, unfazed by her description. He said he could help, but it was necessary to meet beforehand because the procedure was rather complicated; it involved more than just one session, and he needed to explain to his clients exactly how it worked before they could made a decision.

Diana suggested they meet at the Caffè Perù on Via di Monserrato, close to where she lived. It was an old-fashioned bar with a colorful fifties decor—bright tiles and lots of mirrors everywhere—a place that the Rome for Nomads website described as "very popular among hipsters at *aperitivo* time."

When Diana arrived around seven, Caffè Perù was already crowded. People were standing outside with their drinks in hand or placed on the roofs of parked cars. Guys in loose, expensive outfits and girls with heavy eyeliner and dramatic lipstick chatted amiably, smoking cigarettes, laughing, flirting. Definitely a younger crowd, she noticed, looking at ease, as if they had all just come from some interesting gallery opening and were pausing before heading toward another cocktail party. Diana quickly walked inside, feeling slightly left out.

"Diana?"

A man in a vintage fatigue shirt raised a hand from his spot at the bar. Diana had expected Ivo to be a slightly more romantic character. She had pictured him tall and muscular, with an interesting nose, and a shock of dark curls, a man who had lived in the Italian countryside and the Canadian woods. But Ivo was probably in his mid-forties, with a ruddy complexion, a beer belly and a bald patch on his head. They shook hands and he gestured for her to sit next to him on the high stool at the bar. He ordered a Diet Coke, she a mojito. Diana was excited: walking into a bar to meet up with a stranger to discuss a problem concerning her life in Rome was finally giving her a sense of purpose.

At first Ivo spoke in a rather impersonal tone, as if he were reciting a lecture he knew by heart. He said it was going to be a slow process. He would have to come at least two or three times a week.

"Driving out the gulls isn't going to happen in a day; those birds are diehards and sometimes they fight back in groups."

He paused and took a sip of his Diet Coke.

"It is going to be expensive," he added.

"How much?" she asked.

He told her the figure. It was a lot, but she could afford it.

And besides, something told her it was going to be worth it. Not so much because it would allow her use of the terrace, but because she felt very strongly that it was going to be an adventure. Moreover, she sensed it was a way to exercise her power, perhaps a battle she could win. And as such, it was exactly what she needed.

Suddenly Diana started seeing seagulls everywhere.

At daybreak, the cawing started, its chorus resonating throughout the city, like a call to prayer. In the grayish light of dawn she watched their silhouettes perched on the slanting roofs and terraces they had elected to make their homes. At night, as she walked along the Via dei Fori Imperiali, flocks of them swirled above the beams that illuminated the ruins. They fluttered like moths around a lamp; lit from below, their wings acquired a golden glow so that they looked like fleeting ghosts against the blackness of the sky.

———

Women had been openly flirting with Mark throughout the years they'd been a couple, even when Diana was standing right next to him, holding a drink, with her wedding ring in plain sight. She was pretty in a harmless way: devoid of mystery or complexity. Her skin was too white, her eyes too blue, her freckles too childlike, her body too soft. She knew that as soon as she turned her back, the women in the room would ask themselves how was it possible that she, of all people, was the wife of such a sexy, successful man. An architect who looked like a film star? Diana came from some money—was that the reason? The women—younger, older—flirting so openly with Mark didn't think her worthy of their respect.

During the first few years in their marriage, Diana thought of herself as someone who'd won the lottery. This lanky, dark-haired prince with chiseled features, who designed modernist office spaces and iconic restaurants, had chosen *her*. Yet, how long did his passionate love for her last? Six years? Four? When did the sweet notes stuck on the fridge stop coming, the birth-day presents, when did the sex taper off? When did he become moody and bored?

The affair with the redhead had been his first, around five years back. She was a regular guest at mutual friends' din-ner parties, an advertising executive who was also a singer in an indie band, with a hoarse voice and a posh British accent. She was always dressed in bright solid colors and high heels, her fiery copper hair piled up on top of her head like Monica Vitti in an Antonioni movie. She wasn't afraid to drink or smoke too much. She would be somehow antagonistic, then suddenly aloof, and always ended up having the best punch line, in a way that made her quite irresistible. Mark invariably managed to maneuver his way next to her at the dinner table, or to join her by the window for a smoke and chat with her about European films or English rock bands. He had a habit of speaking in whispers to women he liked, so that his interlocu-tor was compelled to lean over to him in order to hear. It was a commanding gesture, to force that closeness on someone, like saying, Come to me; I know you want to. He'd done it with Diana the first time they'd met. She had to lean so close to him, she could smell the warmth of his neck.

Diana remembered standing up in the kitchen in the mid-dle of the night while Mark was asleep, reading his messages to the redhead on his phone. Their words were so hot, so sexy, that she broke into a cold sweat, her heart thumping wildly.

Mark hadn't even bothered to delete their exchanges; probably he didn't think she would have the guts to spy on him.

It wasn't clear how the affair had ended; probably the redhead had been the one to break it off—she didn't seem the type to linger in a situation where she wasn't in complete control. Diana never said a word and swallowed her angst. Mark seemed sad and depleted for a couple of months, and Diana nursed his sadness, without asking anything. She told herself that the affair had been just a hitch, an accident that married people were meant to overcome, a price to pay in exchange for the safety of conjugal life.

A few years of dull, unexciting peace followed, until the young girl on the bicycle made her entrance in the neighborhood.

———

Diana shopped for expensive snacks in the *salumeria* Roscioli on Via dei Giubbonari: jumbo cashew nuts, dried figs from Calabria, a special mozzarella from Bari, cubes of pecorino and aged Parmesan, walnut bread. She arranged the morsels in small bowls, and pulled out a bottle of wine from the fridge. The idea was to greet Ivo with a little something. For some reason she thought that his intervention could be preceded by a quick *aperitivo*. Ivo showed up at her door in an elaborate multipocketed hunting jacket, panting and sweating after five flights of stairs. He was carrying a rectangular aluminum case that looked like a safe.

He pulled out a worn leather glove from one of his many pockets and opened the safe. A hawk hopped gently onto his fist.

"This is Queen," he said. "My lady."

The bird was wearing a weathered leather hood that covered her eyes. It was a beautiful object: hand-stitched with two straps jutting out on each side and a small tassel on the top. It resembled the helm of a warrior, something out of the Crusades, and it gave the bird an almost mythical appearance.

"What's that for?" Diana asked.

"The hood? It helps her to relax and not fly away before I'm ready."

Queen's plumage was a deep chocolate-brown mixed with plush rust-colored feathers. Her taut, compact body tensed, then she snapped her wings with a click, like someone flicking a fan open, and began to move her head in quick, nervous jerks from right to left and left to right. Tiny bells tied around her legs made a tinkling, cheerful sound.

"Please don't move too fast," Ivo warned Diana. "She has to get used to you and the surroundings."

Ivo removed the hood by taking one drawstring in his teeth and pulling the other between thumb and forefinger. Diana flinched as the hawk made an attempt to fly off, throwing herself headlong from Ivo's fist. Two straps fastened around her legs—Ivo explained they were called jesses—were tied to a short leash hooked inside the glove, and held the bird upside down. There was a frenzied jingling of bells and thrashing of plumage, as if the bird were having a hysterical convulsion, but Ivo calmly raised his arm up until the bird managed to pull herself back onto the glove. Ivo brushed the bird with his palm until she slowly quieted down. Her feathers rearranged themselves, rustling like papers.

"Good—she's rousing. It means she's happy," Ivo said, patting her.

Queen locked eyes with Diana with an intimidating, reptilian stare. A completely unexpected sensation shook Diana's blood. This creature was so much more bewildering than she had anticipated.

"She's beautiful," she said in a whisper, unable to find a proper word to describe her.

"Let's get to work," Ivo said and walked toward the French door, ignoring the expensive snacks displayed on the table.

The minute Queen was outside, she pulled at the straps, wanting to take off again.

"What happens now?" Diana asked with anticipation.

"You'll see."

Ivo undid the hook and off she went, like a smooth missile, gliding in the air. There was sudden chaos in the sky; the gulls started their warning calls immediately and, along with them, pigeons, crows and sparrows fluttered away overhead.

"See?" Ivo said, pointing at Queen shooting in a seamless line toward the gulls and the smaller birds. In just a handful of seconds, they dispersed.

"She's beginning to do her job," he continued, keeping his eyes on the bird like a proud parent.

"Gulls know a bird of prey; they see its shape in the sky and immediately recognize it, even though they may have never seen one. It's inscribed in their DNA."

Queen soared in circles, pushing the gulls farther away till the sky above the roof was almost clear of them. The fugitive birds' ruckus was hardly audible now.

"What is she going to . . ." Diana hesitated. "I mean, is she going to kill them now?"

Ivo kept his eyes on the hawk for a few seconds, seemingly more interested in her flight than in Diana's question.

"In this specific situation the gulls are too many and she won't go for it. And we don't want that to happen; we just want to scare them away till they leave for good. But yes, in a different circumstance she would."

He had started to speak in a tone one would use in a lecture.

"Hawks are predators—their instinct is to kill."

"Right."

"Falconry is an ancient art. That's how people put food on the table before they had guns."

"What's the difference, exactly, between a falcon and a hawk, then?" she asked nonchalantly.

"Both are raptors," Ivo replied, his eyes still fixed on his bird. "Difference in size, wing shape, beak, flight pattern. Beginners can't really tell, but with time, one can tell at a glance."

"Of course," Diana said. She wanted to make sure Ivo knew she had done some homework, and that she was ready for anything.

Queen landed on the edge of a roof right across the street. The sky was completely clear.

"Wow," Diana whispered, almost to herself.

"Yes, she's a good hunter. One of the best I've ever had." Ivo was standing with his arms crossed over his paunch and legs slightly parted.

The bird remained still, like a guardian looking out for enemies. Her profile, the sharpness of her beak, was clear cut against the sky.

"Do you actually go hunting with her?" Diana asked.

"Yes, of course. I have to."

"Where do you take her?"

"It depends. Sometimes I drive just half an hour out of town. But I'm not the hunter, I'm only her assistant." Ivo flashed a grin. "My job is to scare a rabbit or a mouse out of the brush so she can kill it. That's the beauty of training a hawk."

"It must be amazing to see her catch prey," Diana said, although she wasn't sure why she thought so.

Ivo's face lit up.

"It's incredible. When hawks approach their prey, you hear it before you see it." Ivo made a loud wheezing sound, like a sharp whistle that ended in a crash. "The shape of their beaks is designed to snap the vertebra and it kills them instantly."

He suddenly became even more animated.

"To have a relationship with an animal that recognizes you as its partner—it's a miracle. I don't know how to explain it. It makes you part of something bigger."

Diana nodded, entranced. She looked up at the sky. Some of the gulls seemed to be returning. A few of them were circling again, not too far from the terrace, as though they were inspecting whether their enemy had left. "They're back. What happens now?"

"I'm going to fly her a few more times today, and we'll keep repeating the flights at least three times a week until the gulls understand that she's taken over their territory. Only then will they move for good. I told you, it may take up to a month—it depends."

"Really? That long?"

"Yes, this is a long procedure. Animals learn by repetition. You'll have to be patient," he added with a tinge of reproach.

Diana immediately rushed to justify herself.

"Oh, no, I'm not impatient at all, quite the contrary. . . . Actually, I'm interested . . . actually thrilled to be watching what she does. I was just curious as to what . . ."

But Ivo wasn't really listening. His eyes were on Queen, who was still perched on the roof across the street, preening. He called her name once, twice, his voice sharp as a bird's call, and she swooped down, landing on his glove like an arrow on target. She began to peck at something bloody that Ivo was holding between his gloved fingers.

"What's that?"

"A chick."

Diana winced.

"Are you serious?"

"Yes," Ivo said, unconcerned. "Hawks are trained to eat from our hand—food is what bonds them to the falconer. That's how they learn to fly back to the fist."

"Where do you get them? The chicks, I mean."

"In the city I have to buy them in batches in a pet shop and keep them in my freezer," he said, then patted a large pocket on his hunting jacket. "This is full of meat. When she's eaten enough we'll stop flying her, because when she has a full belly it's harder to get her back on the glove."

Ivo flew Queen a few more times. Each time the gulls attempted to return but the minute they saw her circling over the terrace, they scattered away again. The hawk always responded to Ivo's call and flew obediently to his fist whenever he called her. He kept pulling out lumps of meat from his vest and hiding them inside the folds of the glove. A feathered chick, a chunk of turkey neck. His fingers were smeared in blood. Whenever Queen flew back to his fist and began to peck at the raw meat, Diana saw something primal, a sort of telepathic connection between the man and the bird. Ivo's gestures were ancient; they had a certain nobility. He told her that hawks could be trained but not domesticated, they were truly a wild thing. The hawks that he flew today were trained in exactly the same way they'd been thousands of years ago.

"What if she doesn't come back? Did that ever happen?" Diana asked.

Ivo smiled. He seemed genuinely cheered by her questions.

"Every time you release a hawk for a hunt, there's a chance you'll never see it again. A few times I had to spend hours in the woods begging Queen to fly back to me. She had eaten too much and just wanted to go to sleep on a branch. Sometimes, if it was getting dark, I had to go home and come back at daybreak to look for her with radio tracking."

"That must've made you pretty anxious."

"Well . . . falconers do lose their birds, you know. It's part of the risk you take when you handle a wild bird. Every hunt could be your last, so you pay attention. It's all about trust. If they want to fly away, they fly away, and there's nothing you can do. It's always the bird's choice to come back."

Something about this phrase resonated deeply with Diana. It was all about trust, a risk one had to take.

"Did you ever lose one?"

"It happened," Ivo admitted wistfully. "And yes, that was tough."

It was beginning to get dark and the air was cooling off. Ivo called Queen back for the last time, and after she flew to him, he patted her wings.

"Good girl, good girl, time to say good night now."

He slipped the hood back on over her head and Queen immediately went still and hopped inside her metal box. Diana caught a sour whiff as she escorted him to the door.

It was Ivo. He smelled of raw meat.

———

In the following days Diana was possessed by a new fever. Something new had ruptured her quiet routine. She couldn't quite name it yet, but it was like being in love again. She waited impatiently for Ivo to come back, but the love object wasn't him. It was the hawk she wanted to see, to understand. To touch.

She no longer went for a run in the morning, forgot to buy food at the market and deserted the kitchen. She abandoned the novel completely now as well and used the laptop only to read whatever she could find out about hawks. She downloaded a book on falconry and watched a documentary about the Arab sheiks who bought hawks for astronomical sums at live auctions and flew them in the desert. Tended by servants, the sheiks camped at night in futuristic tents lit by bright neon lights and decorated with carpets and traditional fabrics. As they waited for the first light of day, they lay on carpets in their pristine, perfectly ironed tunics and white headdresses, each one lost in the screen of his phone. There was a scene where the sheiks were sitting cross-legged around a roasted sheep placed on a mound of rice and served on a silver plate. The men pulled and tore the meat off the bones with their hands and ate avidly, in a similar way to their hawks. In one scene, one of the men invited another to eat the heart. It had been reserved for this one sheik, perhaps because of his higher rank. Diana watched the man rip the heart from the rib cage. It was as big as a child's fist, and the man bit into it.

———

Like most people living in big cities, she had never been interested in the avian world and its activity, but now, thanks to Ivo and his visits with Queen, she began to pay attention. He told her stories about the many other kinds of birds who lived in the city, and Diana began to walk around with her head turned upward.

The sky turned out to be such a busy universe. There was always something going on, unbeknownst to most people who walked beneath it, Ivo said. All one had to do was look up: birds fell in love, mated, competed, built nests, traveled south, stopped to refuel, to rest or to build a permanent home. Ivo told her about the Villa Doria Pamphili Park, up on the Gianicolo hill, how it had turned into a tropical oasis. A few parakeets, imported by pet shops from faraway countries, had escaped from their cages, found a home among its forest of maritime pines and reproduced exponentially. They had doubled in size and got stronger and bolder thanks to their regained freedom. Now the park was filled with their loud chittering and the constant flutter of bright-green feathers zooming from branch to branch. Then there were the starlings—swarms of them flew every evening in beautiful formations over the Tiber. According to Ivo, they flew into the city when nights got too cold in the countryside. To them, the light, the heat of people and traffic felt like a room with a fireplace to gather in. Diana watched them glide over the river at dusk and land on the plane trees along the Tiber. They kept calling one another, making sure not to leave anyone behind, and quieted down only when everyone was in place, like noisy children just before the light is turned off.

The sky over Rome was a highway teeming with life. A vast territory that gave Diana a sense of relief, unlike the ruins, the buried chambers, the underground catacombs. Her gaze had lifted and she felt light, energetic and somehow hopeful— although she wasn't sure what exactly she was hoping for.

———

More than two weeks had gone by, and despite Ivo's interventions, the gulls on the terrace hadn't budged yet. Every time Diana attempted to walk out on the terrace, she heard their cawing, more aggressive than ever. At the end of another day of flights, she decided to confront Ivo.

"I'm just wondering . . ." she asked. "Could it be that Queen isn't aggressive enough, in this case?"

They were sitting at the table in the kitchen. Ivo had placed the hawk back into her box, hooded and ready to go into sleep mode.

He seemed annoyed by her question.

"That's not the point."

By now Ivo had become used to Diana and was no longer so awkward around her. After Queen's last flight of the day he would accept the Diet Coke she kept in the fridge especially for him. He had even yielded to her expensive refreshments. Feeding him had become a matter of principle for Diana, as though her objective was, snack by snack, to tame him, just as he had done with his bird.

She was getting used to him too. The dirt encrusted on

his fingernails, the pungent smell emanating from his body, the blotchy and reddish skin, his grimy clothes, no longer troubled her. Despite all of that—or was it thanks to that?—Ivo carried within himself a kind of medieval energy that redeemed his looks.

"The thing is she's alone against a large group," he said, slowly lifting another Parmesan cube. "She needs to guard her back."

Then he gestured toward the window.

"You see how she goes out and scares them off but after she flies back she always sits against a wall? She's thinking strategically: she knows they could come back in force and attack her from different directions—that's how clever she is. She makes sure she always has her back covered on one side."

Diana nodded.

"Right. That's very smart."

"I told you that it would take time to drive them out. We're almost there."

There was a brief silence.

"It's spring already and I haven't been able to have lunch on my terrace once," Diana said. "How much longer do you think, realistically?"

Ivo scratched his chin.

"Let me put it this way. If I brought Darko they'd work as a team and look after each other's back. And that would be a completely different scene."

"Darko?"

He paused and took a sip of his soda.

"My peregrine falcon. He's three years old and a very challenging hunter. Peregrine falcons are the fastest animals on earth."

"So why don't we?"

"It's not a good idea."

"Why?"

He paused and wouldn't answer. She raised her eyebrows quizzically.

"It's not a clean job," he said finally.

"How so?"

Ivo put down his glass and wiped his mouth with the back of his hand. He stood up, ready to go.

"There might be blood."

Diana felt a thrill move along her spine. The idea of two predators reclaiming the territory on her behalf excited her beyond any expectation. But maybe this was wrong, maybe she was supposed to renounce her plan in order to avoid collateral damage.

"What exactly do you mean by that?" she asked in a guardedly casual way.

Ivo collected his leather jacket from the back of the chair and slowly put it on. "You can't predict what will happen. What I'm saying is once my birds are together and feel safe enough, they will go all out."

He paused again.

"They'll go for the kill, is what I mean."

Diana tilted her head slightly on one side and nodded slowly.

"And when there's blood, then that's it. Bam, gulls are gone for good."

There was another silence.

"I see," Diana said at last. "And . . . ?"

"Technically it would be illegal," Ivo continued. "Gulls are a protected species. It's one thing for Queen to herd them away, another for Darko to—"

Ivo stopped himself in midsentence, grabbed Queen's carrier box and made for the door.

"Don't be ridiculous, Ivo. Gulls in this city are pests. It says so all over the internet," Diana said forcefully. She felt by now she had gained the right to call them that. "We are the ones who should be protected from them!"

"I know. But that's the way it is. I didn't make that law. You'll just have to be patient."

He gave Diana a look that meant *Say no more* and closed the door behind him.

Maybe gulls did have a redeeming quality, after all. They mated for life—she remembered reading that on her first online search—and they were considered one of the most loyal species in the animal world. So, what was she doing, thinking of hiring a killer?

But whatever instinct had stirred in Diana since Queen's arrival, it wasn't going away. She knew she had entered a new realm and that something tectonic in her world was about to shift.

———

Diana and Mark continued to speak on the phone every day, like students grudgingly doing their homework. She could tell Mark was always doing something else while talking to her. Different sounds betrayed different activities. Either he was making himself a sandwich, watching TV or working on his computer. Once she even heard a toilet flush. Their conversations were becoming more and more unfocused. Diana had attempted to revive his interest by telling him about her adventures with Ivo and Queen. She wanted him to admire her ingenuity and resolve, maybe to be concerned about her safety, or simply to be excited about the hawk. But he sounded removed, as though all that was happening in Rome were a blur and irrelevant to him. He told her he had been suffering with a particularly severe headache, which he described as a cold blade cutting his brain into very thin slices. He had gone to see an Ayurvedic doctor, who told him he was depleted and needed to revive some of his *pitta.*

"What's that?" Diana asked.

"*Pitta* is 'heat' in Ayurveda. Apparently I've lost my inner fire."

That felt like an accusation, as if Diana had something to do with this loss. Later that night she kept turning in bed, wondering what exactly she was going back to in three weeks, when she returned to New York.

Once Mark regained his fire he'd fall again for someone else—it was inevitable. Probably his previous affairs hadn't worked out because his choices had been poor, but what would stop him the minute someone new, and with a charming sense of humor, appeared?

She was going back to a languishing experiment, an inert agreement. Someone had to be brave and pull the plug.

She processed this concept for a while. Then one morning she woke up, steadfast. The message was absolutely clear, as if it had come to her from a loudspeaker.

To pull the plug was an act of mercy. It meant relieving Mark by taking on the job he didn't want to do. It would only enable him to rise again from whatever ailment had flattened him so that his so-called *pitta* could give new fuel to his narcissism. No, that's not what she needed to do. It was the hypocritical pact, the lie, that had to be destroyed for good.

What she needed wasn't mercy; it was more rage.

———

It was April and the daffodils were in full bloom on Diana's terrace; on weekends the young crowd sat in the sun outside Caffè Perù, and Ivo was feeling optimistic. At the end of another flying day he announced the gulls were beginning to lose hold of their territory. There were only a few left.

"One or two more interventions and they'll be gone for good."

Diana should have been relieved. But she wasn't. She wanted more drama. The nest, she felt, had to be completely destroyed. It had become her mission, and she needed to see it fulfilled now and to the end. A grand finale, that's what she longed for.

Diana watched Ivo walk down the nautilus staircase holding Queen's carrier. He had almost reached the third floor when she leaned over the bannister and called his name. His footsteps came to a halt as her voice echoed down the marble stairs.

"I want the peregrine falcon," she commanded. "Bring Darko."

———

It was dusk. Queen flew out first, then Ivo released Darko. He was bulkier, his plumage a lighter blue-gray. He was scarier, with his stare mad and feral. He soared behind Queen and Diana could feel a new determination in their flight, as though both birds knew they were going in for the kill. She watched Darko draw his wings back and turn into a streamlined shape that cut through the air like a rocket. The gulls were scattering more quickly than she'd ever seen them do before, sending warning cries all around them. In just a few seconds Darko climbed higher than Queen, until he became a tiny spot in the sky. Ivo grabbed Diana by the arm and pressed his fingers around her wrist in the same way Queen's talons had gripped his glove. She was surprised by his touch but she realized they too had become a team now.

"See? He needs to attack from above in order to gain speed and surprise while Queen distracts them," he said, entranced.

Diana held her breath. She felt how Ivo had switched on his telepathic connection with the hawks; she sensed an almost shamanic transformation come over her. Half bird, half human herself, she squinted into the last rays of the sun that was setting behind the river, zeroing in on Queen circling in the air as she pushed the gulls a bit farther away. Then, before either Diana or Ivo could perceive his intent, Darko opened his wings and began a steep descent from way up in the sky.

"Here we go. Watch him now," Ivo said under his breath, tightening his grip on her wrist.

It took no time.

A final lunge, a supersonic dive and in one sweep Darko seized a gull in the clutch of his claws. Then a crash not far from where Ivo and Diana were standing.

Darko, followed closely by Queen, landed with his prey. With synchronized precision and focus, they started tearing at the gull, just as Ivo had predicted. There was the sound of thin bones snapping, white plumes floating, a burst of dark red. The gull was still alive, still wailing, raucously.

Diana closed her eyes for a moment and listened to the frenzied flapping of wings, the cracking of ribs, the desperate cawing. She conjured the bird's blood staining the terra-cotta tiles.

She had read, in one of the books on falconry, how there is a moment when the falconer's bloodlust vanishes, along with his connection with the hawk, and the hunter suddenly returns to being human. It was precisely at that instant, Diana realized, that the hunter's rage must turn to mercy—to help the prey die fast.

When Diana opened her eyes again she saw Ivo crouching between his hawks, reaching down between the flailing feathers, giving the gull its coup de grâce. A contraction in her chest, and she sighed with release: his job was done at last, and so was hers.

Then nothing moved and there was silence.

THE CALLBACK

Julian hadn't been back in Rome for more than twenty-five years, not since he was a boy. Nobody in his family had ever wished to return. Given what had happened there, the city had become an enemy.

At first, coming in from the airport, Julian was shocked to find himself on the same streets that once had been so familiar but that he now hardly recognized. Potholes, rabid drivers, graffiti everywhere, trash piled on the sidewalks, a general sense of doom. The city had radically changed, as if throughout the years whoever had been in charge had stopped caring, like an heirless aristocrat who no longer has the money or inclination to maintain his family palazzo and is waiting only for the roof to collapse once and for all.

Romans had changed as well, and for good reasons. The whole country was entangled in a financial crisis that had started ten years earlier, and its glorious capital was in rags. Angry and hostile, the people of Rome had come to despise the tourists who occupied the sidewalks en masse, marching in a stupefied trance behind their guides' tiny flags; they resented the never-ending rattle of the suitcases being wheeled over the cobblestones and the defrosted packaged meals the invaders were made to eat in cheap trattorias designed to poison them.

The producers of his movie had made sure to protect Julian from any kind of potential discomfort by putting him in one of the best hotels near Piazza del Popolo. A driver in uniform would be on hand 24/7 to take him wherever he wished to go, safely sealed behind tinted windows. They made sure the car was stocked with plenty of Evian bottles, light snacks, a fresh copy of *The New York Times* and classical music queued up on Spotify.

———

Valeria was asked to wait in the lounge area across from reception.

The production office looked like a boutique hotel: the lights were strategically dimmed, walls had been painted a dark, rich red. Between a couple of striped armchairs, issues of *Variety* and *The Hollywood Reporter* were spread fanlike on the low table. A sad song of an indie band she liked was coming through the speakers on low volume. She was offered a glass of water with a slice of lemon and a mint leaf.

She'd gotten a callback. The casting director had told her it was a good sign, as so far nobody had been asked to come back for that role. He told Valeria that over the weekend Julian Johnson had been watching all the auditions on his iPad, and he had asked to meet her. It was going to be only a short interview, more like a conversation. Mr. Johnson had also requested to see her with blond hair. Would that be possible? They had already scheduled an appointment with a colorist on Tuesday. The production would pay, of course.

This was the part of being an actress she resented most, how it allowed total strangers to make decisions that involved her body, as if it had become their property overnight. Lose weight, gain weight, cut hair, whiten your teeth, stop shaving under armpits, change eye color with contact lenses, fill that line with Botox. She was in her early forties and had been sent for Botox injections more than once already.

The previous day, in the hair salon, once they had given her a last touch after the blow-dry and massaged in a drop of oily product for shine, the hairdresser and his two assistants clustered behind her and cooed through the mirror.

"You look amazing."

"This color totally suits you."

"You look ten years younger."

She hated herself as a blonde. She thought she looked fake—and ridiculous.

The role was small and not interesting. The character she auditioned for was somebody's wife—mostly silent, since in all of her scenes the men did most of the talking—but, besides the fact that she needed to work, she was in awe of Julian Johnson. He was such an interesting director, and although his movies had modest budgets and were independent, he often worked with great actors who didn't care about the money because they loved his work. This was the first time he was shooting a movie in Italy, and the buzz in Rome had been hysterical. Every single actor she knew had been dying to get an audition.

An assistant appeared and in a quiet whisper asked her to follow him.

————

"Valeria, so nice to meet you."

Valeria's heart thumped as Julian Johnson shook her hand. He stared at her intently—or maybe he was just assessing her new hair color; it was difficult to tell. He gestured at an armchair.

"Thanks for coming. Please, have a seat."

Thanks for coming? Valeria thought. As if it had been a favor on her part to show up, as if she didn't desperately want the role and didn't need the prestige, let alone the money. Americans were so used to their scripted greetings, they didn't realize how artificial they could sound. But at least they made the effort, unlike Italians, who were curt and unfriendly whenever they had the upper hand and hardly ever attempted to make you feel welcome.

Johnson looked more mature than in the photos. Though he probably was only a few years younger than Valeria, he already had a significant streak of gray around his temples. But he was skinny and taut and wore a sweatshirt over his jeans like a street kid.

"I really liked your audition. Your English is very good," he said. "You have almost no accent."

"Thank you."

She reminded herself to speak slowly, to keep breathing, take a relaxed posture while sitting, and not to smirk or giggle.

"In fact, maybe you'll need to fake a bit of an inflection for the part. I want the character to sound more Italian."

"Okay. No problem with that."

Did that mean he'd already made up his mind? Was she in?

"Where did you learn your English?" he asked.

"Oh . . . in my twenties I lived in Los Angeles for a couple of years." Then she shrugged, as if to justify herself. "Acting school and waitressing, like everyone else."

"But you came back to live here."

"Yes. I thought I'd have a better chance to act in my own language. Even though my accent is light I still sound like a foreigner. In Los Angeles I could audition only for Latinas, Italians or Greeks. Plus I didn't have a work permit."

"That makes sense."

He was looking at a sheet of paper.

"I see you've done a lot of theater here."

She nodded.

"And some TV," he said.

"Some bad TV, I'm afraid."

He smiled and put the sheet away.

"Don't worry. A lot of good actors end up in bad shows; it's not their fault. My assistant showed me a couple of scenes on YouTube from that crime series you were in."

"Oh, no."

"Why? You're good. I couldn't understand much because my Italian isn't as fluent as it once was."

That sounded like an invitation to ask him about how he had learned it.

"Do you speak Italian?" she asked.

"Un poco. Ma ora ho dimenticato quasi tutto."

His accent was thick, but Valeria encouraged him.

"Non è vero, hai un buonissimo accento."

"No, I don't. And I forgot most of it. My family moved to Rome for three years when I was about nine."

"Really? How come?"

"My father worked for FAO, the food and agriculture organization of the UN."

Valeria felt the conversation was veering away from the reason she had come—her character, the audition, the hair. But this friendliness was a good sign, she thought. She hadn't expected that he would be so chatty and relaxed.

"And where did you live?" she asked.

"Near the Aventino. My sister and I went to the international school nearby."

She hesitated, imperceptibly.

"Saint Stephen's?"

"Yes. You've heard of it?"

Valeria shifted in her seat.

"Yes. . . . I mean . . . I know where it is."

"It's a small school—not many people know it."

"Well," Valeria said uneasily, eager to get back to the previous conversation, "I guess Rome feels pretty familiar, then. It must be nice to be back here to shoot a movie."

"Yes and no," he said, and for a split second he paused as if he had lost his line of thought. "We left right after Maya . . ."

He shook his head lightly, looking away, as though he wanted to backtrack from whatever he was about to say.

"Maya?" Valeria's voice cracked as she repeated the name.

They looked at each other, and for a handful of seconds they remained silent. Valeria felt the density of the air around them begin to alter, till she felt it pressing on her chest.

"Yes. My older sister. She was in a . . ." Julian's voice faded as he attempted to complete the phrase.

Valeria stared at him, without answering. Her face had turned ashen, and her whole body had stiffened.

He studied her more closely. "Are you okay?" he asked, then stopped himself. Suddenly his expression changed too, as if a blinding flash had erased everything he had been thinking about till then.

"You are . . . ?" he started, then put his elbows on the table and rested his face behind his hands.

"What?" she said.

He raised his head. His features had softened; he was more permeable now, had lost the formal mask of courtesy and seemed younger, almost boyish.

Valeria started to shoot frantic glances all around the room, while Julian closed his eyes for a moment. Then their voices merged, crossing over each other.

"Are you . . . ?"

"Oh God."

"Sorry, I know this is crazy."

"No, it's not."

"Are you *that* Valeria?"

Blood started rushing through her—she felt it flowing in her wrists, in her throat. Her head was spinning. So she bent over and this time it was her turn to cover her face with her hands.

"Oh God," she repeated.

"I'm sorry," Julian said. "I didn't know. When I asked to see you again . . . Believe me, I had absolutely no—"

"No, I . . . I mean *now*, how . . . how did you . . . ?"

"I just had a feeling. I don't know why. Suddenly I knew it was you. When I mentioned her name, your expression . . . I just *knew.*"

She couldn't hide anymore, so she lowered her hands. Her eyes were moist, her cheeks flushed.

"No. It's okay. It's just that . . . it was so unexpected. You caught me completely off guard."

Julian seemed lost, his body slumped on the chair.

"I can't believe this is happening," he said.

———

So this is you, he thought.

You've been just a name for all these years, like a character in a novel. *The* bad character, in fact. And now here you are, in this cheap coat, with the lifeless hair I asked you to bleach in a color that doesn't suit you. You are taller than I expected, you have thick eyebrows, light eyes and small hands that keep fidgeting. You are that name. Valeria.

Julian watched her as she heaved and leaned with her head toward her knees as though she might black out.

"Can I have a glass of water, please?" she whispered.

———

Apparently, the actress in Julian's office was having something akin to a panic attack, the receptionist told the assistant director, a young woman with a mass of curly blond hair and round glasses, who ran into the room in order to relieve Julian from this inconvenience. She escorted the actress to the restroom so she could splash her face with cold water. Valeria

kept shaking and saying she was sorry while Julian stood outside the bathroom, distraught. He knocked on the bathroom
door a couple of times.

"Is she okay? Shall we call a doctor?"

When the two women came out, the assistant noticed how
his face had undergone a drastic transformation in the space
of a few minutes: his features had collapsed like a sandcastle
smashed by a wave.

Julian insisted that somebody drive Valeria home. There
were a couple of drivers on hand, but she said no, she just
needed to be outside, she wanted to walk.

"I'm okay now," she said to him, and turned to the assistant
director. "I'll be fine, I promise. I just need to breathe and be
alone."

After she left, Julian sank into a chair in the middle of the
office corridor. The assistant director asked him if he needed
anything and he said she should cancel whatever meetings
were scheduled for the rest of the day because he was heading
back to the hotel.

———

Julian had a suite. Cushions in muted colors were scattered
on the couch, thick bunches of pale hydrangea matched the
faded pink and mauve of the room, candles spread a sweet
scent. He had taken half a Xanax two hours earlier and canceled dinner with the Italian film distributor, but the night
felt like a never-ending threat stretched in front of him. He
dialed a number on his phone.

"Hi . . ."

"Who is it?"

"It's me, Mom. Julian."

"Oh God, Jules . . . I didn't recognize your voice, you sound so hoarse. Did you catch a cold on the flight?"

"No."

"What are you doing awake at this time? Isn't it the middle of the night over there?"

"It's not late—it's just after ten," Julian said impatiently.

When he had told his mother that his next film would be set partly in Rome she had seemed disappointed, as if he had been in some way disloyal to her and the rest of the family.

"What's the weather like over there?" she asked. "I saw it's been raining a lot."

"It stopped. It's spring again. Listen—"

"Your brother is in town with the children," she interrupted him. "They're coming to lunch on Sunday and—"

"Mom?"

"Yes?"

Julian took a long breath.

"I met Valeria today."

"Who?"

He wasn't sure how to answer. There were verbs and specific words he needed to avoid, although his mother probably already knew who he was talking about and was only buying seconds.

He cleared his throat.

"Maya's Valeria."

"Oh, no," she said very slowly. Then he heard a slow exhale, like thin air hissing out of a balloon.

"She's an actress now. My casting director called her for a small role and today she came to the office. We were just talking and suddenly, somehow . . ."

He stopped. His mother remained silent.

Julian had an ability to decipher the different nature of silences. Some were innocent, full of expectation and longing. Others were dark, filled with resentment. Some felt like marble, like this one. He could picture his mother retracting and curling in alarm. The beautiful bony face, the straight hair parted in the middle—the immortal Joan Didion style she had worn since her twenties and had never changed. He heard a rustling sound and figured she must be reaching for a cigarette with the lightly warped, arthritic fingers that always pained her in the mornings. He pictured the familiar gold ring in the shape of a knot she wore on her index finger. She couldn't take it off anymore because of the knuckle swelling.

"Somehow?" she finally repeated.

"I can't explain it—it's a coincidence, pure and simple. I realized who she was in a way that was like . . . a flash. Her name is Valeria, but she had a different last name, so it never occurred to me that she . . . But then, when I mentioned Maya's name, she—"

She cut him short, reproachful. "Stop it. I can't have this conversation now. Not like this, out of the blue."

"I just wanted to let you know."

"Not on the phone, long-distance," she said, raising her voice. "Really, Jules, what's wrong with you?"

Julian threw his head backward, resigned. Of course, he thought—he should have known better. He and his mother had always been incapable of talking fully about Maya. Their grief had turned into a taboo.

"You're right. This is a mistake. Sorry," he said, and wondered if their silence would last forever.

"Don't be sorry. It's just impossible. It's not your fault."

They were both quiet for a few seconds, listening to each other's breathing. Then his mother's bitter voice came up again.

"Jesus. I was hoping I'd never have to hear that name again."

———

It was almost eleven at night. Valeria was standing up by the kitchen counter, eating mechanically from a can of beans, eyes fixed on the tiles by the sink. She had washed her makeup off, tied her hair back with a plastic hair clip and changed into more comfortable clothes, a T-shirt with a cardigan and her blue pajama trousers. She was supposed to be going to a movie with a man she slept with on and off, but she told him she was coming down with a bad cold. Being alone hadn't helped her feel any better. If anything, the weight pressing on her lungs was becoming heavier and heavier. There was nobody she could talk to about what had just happened. There were so many people in her life now who had never even heard the story, and it was too late to tell it. Her brother was in Berlin and they had slowly drifted apart, for no particular reason but geographical distance. Her mother suffered from depression, and was the last person who could help. Her father was dead.

The phone rang.

"Hi. This is Julian."

It took a second for her to realize it was him.

"I got your number from my assistant."

"Yes. Hi."

"Are you okay?"

"Yes, I'm fine now, thank you. I'm so sorry. I didn't mean to break down like that—"

"No need to apologize."

"Yes."

Again, there was a silence. She waited.

"Just in case you were still wondering, I didn't know who you were when I asked the casting director to see you again," he said. "I didn't make the connection. I barely pay attention to the actors' names, but yours didn't sound familiar, anyway. Did you change it?"

Was there a slight accusation in his tone? She couldn't tell.

"I use my mother's last name for work, just because I was told it has a better sound," she said, as if to justify herself. "And I didn't make the connection either. 'Johnson' is such a common name and . . . I didn't remember she had a brother named Julian."

Neither one said anything.

"We need to talk," he finally said.

"Yes, of course."

"If you don't feel like it, however, I'd totally understand."

She paused again, thinking.

"I dread it. But I want to at the same time."

"I know. Yet if you think this is too much——"

"No. I told you—I need to talk about it as well."

"So, let's see. Could you come to my hotel? Are you free?"

"You mean like . . . now?"

"Yes. That would be great."

"Okay."

"I don't want to force you or anything. But I've been think-ing all day about what happened."

"You're not forcing me. Which hotel?" she said briskly. Somehow he no longer intimidated her.

"I think we both need to process this and——"

"I know. Just tell me the name of the hotel and I'll be right over."

"Right. It's the Hotel de Russie. On Via del Babuino."

"I know where it is. I'll be there in half an hour."

———

Valeria arrived in a taxi. She was too agitated to risk another ride in a bus. A man with a top hat and epaulets opened the door of the car for her.

"Welcome to the De Russie, madam," he said in English.

She hadn't bothered to change, and under her coat she was still wearing her old T-shirt and pajama trousers, which could pass for harem pants. It was odd, but it didn't matter anymore what she looked like to Julian; they were meeting for a different reason now, and her priority was to feel like herself as much as possible. It was the only thing that would anchor her, she thought.

She felt awkward asking the concierge to ring Mr. Johnson's room when she looked like she had just gotten out of bed—he might mistake her for a stalker—but the young man at the desk showed no perceptible reaction to the request.

She skirted the gigantic flower arrangement in the lobby and headed toward the bar. Sitting around a couple of low tables were a few burly men in suits surrounded by women in designer clothes. Russians, most probably. Every single item the women wore looked shiny and perfectly pressed, as if it had come straight out of the tissue wrap of an expensive shop around the corner.

———

As he stepped out of the elevator, Julian saw Valeria in a corner of the bar, sitting on the edge of a small sofa, her back stiff and upright, her knees touching. She looked younger now that she was wearing no makeup and her hair was disheveled. He sank into the velvet armchair across from her. He felt wired and exhausted, still in the jeans and sweatshirt he'd been wearing that morning.

"Ciao," he said and ran a hand through his hair.

"Ciao," Valeria answered, equally drained.

He gestured toward a waiter.

"Let's drink. I think we need some help here."

The young man came over to take their order.

"I'm having a Moscow mule," Julian said. "How about you?"

"I'm not sure what that is but I'll have one too."

"Good choice."

"I don't drink much anymore."

"It's vodka, lime and ginger beer. It won't get you drunk. Believe me, a bit of booze is going to make this easier."

The bar was slowly filling up with sparks of laughter and glitter and beautiful people ready to go out somewhere for the later part of the night.

Julian placed his elbows on his knees and leaned toward her.

"I'm not sure what I want to hear from you. I guess I just want to know who you are. Does that make any sense?"

Valeria tugged at her overcoat.

"I don't know," she said. "Does it change anything to know me?"

"No, of course not. Still, you're the other side of a story that belongs to both of us."

Julian could tell Valeria was scared and resentful at the same time, like someone being dragged into a police station for the third-degree. And whether he liked it or not, he was going to be the cop in the interrogation room.

There was a short silence, then he leaned back on the chair and looked up at the ceiling.

"This is insane."

Valeria raised her palms wide open. "Look. My hands are still shaking."

Just then the waiter arrived with their drinks in chunky copper mugs, and put them down. Valeria quickly placed her hands back on her lap. Julian handed her the drink and told her that for some reason a Moscow mule was always served like that, and he had no idea why. While he turned to sign the check, she felt a slight tremor vibrate all over her body, as if her muscles and nerves were no longer attached to her bones. She took a sip, then another.

"It's good. And strong."

The smartly dressed Russians behind them were gathering their things. The women clutched elaborate bags, sparkly and overstudded. They all stood up, laughing, leaving a trail of floral perfume behind them.

"What is it you want me to tell you?" Valeria asked.

Julian cleared his throat.

"I'm not sure. I think I want to hear your version of the story—"

"My version? You mean . . . you want me to tell you how it happened?"

She sounded incredulous. That he—or was it fate?—should summon her, after so many years, to recount the story from her point of view.

He nodded, undeterred by her obvious unease.

Valeria took another sip and then, with deliberation, placed her drink back down on the table. She brushed the rim of the glass with the tip of her finger a couple of times, keeping her eyes down. She felt tears coming and willed them back. She wasn't going to cry.

"Maya was your older sister?"

"Yes. I was just a kid then. I was twelve and she was fifteen."

Valeria kept her eyes still fixed on her glass. Then she looked straight at him, almost defiantly. She spoke, selecting each word with extreme care, as though she kept searching for them, one by one, as she went along.

"I was eighteen. I had just passed my driving test a few months earlier. . . ."

Julian assented, impatient for her to continue.

"It was dark. I was going to a movie. I saw something light flash across the windshield. Her coat, maybe. Then a thud. She had stepped down from the tram platform to cross the street. One step. One second. That was all it took."

Julian suddenly jerked, leaning against the back of the armchair. He crossed his arms behind his head as if he needed some distance from that image. The coat flying across the windshield. It was the green one, he remembered that.

"Wow," he said, and then was quiet. The word *thud* kept echoing and it felt like a blow to the chest.

"Before we moved to Rome we lived in South Africa. We were used to driving on the left side," he said.

"I know. That's what everyone said. That she looked the wrong way before she stepped down from the platform."

Valeria paused. She felt short of breath, all of a sudden. Then she gathered herself and continued.

"There was no way I could've avoided . . ."

She was wary of certain words too. One had to be careful

around verbs that ignited images that one might not be ready to recall.

"Then, I don't know. All I remember is chaos. A big crowd, people screaming, hysteria because the ambulance was taking too long. I was in a trance, I hadn't even begun to realize the entirety of what had just happened. The . . . enormity. I mean, when the ambulance arrived I had no idea whether she was still . . . I thought, I mean, I was hoping with all my heart that she was . . ." She stopped and closed her eyes. "It took only a second. And that second changed my life."

She looked up at him.

"Our lives," she admitted, lowering her gaze again.

———

Julian was only five when he realized, as most everyone does around that age, that his parents probably would die before him. But he was so shocked by this wrenching truth that he was sent to a therapist to help him overcome the anxiety; eventually, at eight, he made peace with it like the rest of humanity has to. But Maya—oh, no—she couldn't disappear; his sister was forever.

They were siblings, they would grow up together, at the same pace, get married and have children after Mom and Dad had been long gone. Eventually they would turn into their parents, drink whiskey on the rocks before dinner, buy expensive clothes, go together to classical music concerts or maybe to Paris. But they would have each other, until the end of time—that was a given. Maya belonged to the same realm as he did, a realm where nobody gets hurt, where nobody dies.

Suddenly there was movement behind Julian's back.

"Excuse me . . ."

A young woman in a bomber jacket embroidered with a big sequined tiger was moving toward them. She had very large dark glasses and powdery pink cropped hair.

"Sorry to disturb you, Julian. I just couldn't help it—I'm such a great fan of your work."

The woman stretched out her hand.

"Hi, my name is Betsy Wagner. I'm Nicholas Reading's stylist. We're here for a *Vogue* shoot. Are you staying at the hotel?"

Julian didn't take her hand.

"Actually, we're in the middle of something," he said icily.

The woman started rummaging inside a tiny handbag strapped on a chain across her shoulder. She fished out a card.

"Of course—forgive my intrusion. Here's my name, or you can ask the concierge for Nicholas's room. I'm sure he'd be stoked to have a drink with you, if you have time, of course. He adores your work. We're here until Friday."

As soon as the woman had left, Julian stood up.

"Do you mind if we go upstairs? I need a bit of peace and quiet and it seems impossible to be left alone in here."

Then he gestured to the waiter and pointed at their empty glasses.

"Could you please send another round to the room? And maybe something to eat, like a couple of club sandwiches with fries."

They had settled down, one across from the other in the small living room, and were speaking quietly, in a kind of verbal slow motion. They didn't touch the food when it arrived because neither one was hungry, but they kept sipping their drinks. Julian was right: the alcohol helped.

"What about your parents? Where were they in all this?" he asked.

"My dad was living in Germany with his new wife and children and we weren't close. My mother lived with her new boyfriend, whom I didn't like. I had left home right after school because it wasn't a healthy situation for me to be in, so I had moved in with a friend, Veronica. We shared a tiny apartment near Piazza Vittorio. I must've called her from a public phone from the street where the accident happened, because I remember her being there with me at some point. She was very practical; she dealt with the ambulance, the police and stuff. At the station I was questioned—I remember there were also a couple of witnesses who gave their version of the accident—but eventually they let us go home. I don't remember what happened to my car—maybe the insurance needed to inspect it—all I know is that Veronica hailed a taxi and I think that's when she told me that Maya was dead. I do remember that moment: the taxi driver wanted us to get out because I was howling so loudly."

Just then Valeria slipped off her shoes and curled up on the sofa. She put a pillow behind her head and closed her eyes. She seemed drunk, or ready to fall asleep. But Julian kept staring forcefully at her, until she reopened them, as if he had managed to call her back to life.

Valeria took another sip of her drink.

"My mother was hopeless. She's not very good at taking

care of people in a crisis. Eventually my father came to Rome and dealt with the lawyers. Everyone kept saying, 'It's not your fault—it was an accident,' but instead of making me feel better, it made me angry. I wanted someone to tell me that it *was* my fault. I wanted the police to come and take me to jail."

Was she trying to buy his forgiveness by saying that? she wondered. It was the truth, yet it sounded so wrong to say this to him, or perhaps wildly inadequate.

"But they didn't," he said.

The words sounded hard, packed with anger, like a stone he had to spit out.

"I always wondered about that, how it is possible . . ." Julian shook his head in disbelief. "I mean, you *kill* someone and . . ." His voice faltered slightly. "And they let you get away? What kind of law allows that?"

Valeria felt again that rush of blood to the nape of her neck, and the internal buzzing resumed. She feared that her body was going to disobey and go crazy again. She made an effort to control her breathing, so that her voice could remain neutral.

"I hadn't had a drink. I was sober. It was dark and I was going slowly, within the speed limit. The witnesses testified that she stepped down from the platform at the very last fraction of a second, when it was impossible for a driver . . . for me to avoid her."

Julian suddenly got up, as if he needed a break, and walked over to the large window that looked out on Via del Babuino. He looked out for a moment, then turned the handle and opened the window. The warm air brushed the flowers in the vase, the flames of the candles. The city sounds immediately infiltrated the room: the low hum of traffic, a distant horn, voices, someone laughing on the street below. This lovely narrow street had changed so much since the time he had lived in the city: he suddenly remembered that there used to be an old bar with wood paneling reeking of cigarette smoke on the opposite side of the hotel. In its place now there was a shop selling what seemed to be cheap sunglasses. At that very moment his phone began to vibrate. He pulled it out of his pocket.

"Sorry—I need to take this."

He walked into the suite's bedroom. He left the door ajar and she could see just a portion of the interior. A plush maroon armchair, white-and-mauve-striped curtains, more flowers. Julian was sitting on the bed with his back to her—she could see only half of him—speaking to someone. Someone he loved, she supposed, at least judging from the intimate tone of his voice. She looked at the time. It was way past midnight already. She felt a strong urge to leave, to get away from him.

After a few minutes he came back into the room, scratching his head. He unlaced his sneakers and sat cross-legged on the opposite side of the couch, facing her. He sat still for a few seconds.

"I'm sorry," Valeria said. "I know hearing all this again must be incredibly difficult."

He didn't answer and lifted the lid that covered the club sandwich, sneaked a glance at the fries and put one in his mouth.

"Want some?"

"No, thanks," Valeria said, even though she was beginning to feel hungry. It felt wrong to eat just then.

"Are you married? Do you have children?" he asked her.

"No. Why are you asking?"

"Just curious." Julian said. "That was my wife. To her Maya

is just a name. Almost an anecdote from my past. I don't think she ever realized how much it affected me to have lost her. I hardly mention Maya to her. I guess one tends to protect people we love from . . ." He made a vague gesture, as if he couldn't find the right word. "Grief, I guess."

"It's difficult to talk to people about something that can't be fixed, that they have no way of soothing," Valeria offered.

Julian nodded, but as if following a new thought. Or maybe he just didn't want to allow her the benefit of agreeing with her.

He faced her. "Did you ever talk to a therapist?" His tone was surgical, devoid of any empathy, as though he didn't want to be implicated in any of her emotions.

"Not at the time. I wanted to get as far as possible from here; I guess I was in total denial. So I left—I moved to Los Angeles, like I told you, and went to acting school for about a year."

Julian stared at her. Again, his expression was impenetrable, but she felt he wasn't satisfied with what she was saying.

Valeria complied. "Basically I ran away."

"Did it help?" Julian asked.

The question was probably meant to sound sarcastic, but she decided to ignore it.

"I saw a therapist years later and that helped, but I'm still terrified to bring it up. Not so much because it pains me but because it's like landing a hand grenade in the middle of a conversation. People get uncomfortable; they freeze. And even when I make the effort and I try to stay honest in telling what happened, each time I feel like an impostor, as if I keep changing the angle according to the person I have in front of me."

"Do you feel you're being an impostor now?"

She held his gaze.

"No."

Julian looked away from her. Valeria waited for him to turn back to her, but he didn't.

"What was she like?" she asked, finally.

Julian gave her a blank stare.

"Maya. What kind of person was she?" Valeria insisted. "I don't think I ever saw a picture, or if I did, I think I have made myself forget it."

"She was . . ." He hesitated and looked away for a moment. For the first time his eyes lit up. "Very beautiful and very funny. She had that deadpan humor that I always tried to imitate but couldn't really. And she was smart. She wanted to be an archaeologist, learn Sanskrit, go to India. I wish I'd known her as an adult. What hurts me the most now is that I'll never be able to talk to her as an equal, ask her advice or show her my work, for instance. Or know what hers would turn out to be. But I know we'd have so much in common."

Julian picked up his phone from the low table between them and started punching the screen and scrolling through images.

"Here," he said under his breath and handed her the cell.

"Maya, my younger brother and me in Sicily. The last summer we spent together. She had just turned fifteen."

It was a shot of a crinkled photograph on paper, probably enlarged. The margins were blurred. Two boys and a girl, slightly taller than her brothers, standing in front of the ruins of an ancient temple. Maya was in the middle, the tallest of the three, looking at her feet. Valeria couldn't make out her face very well.

"She had just met this Italian boy in Rome and they were in love. I think it was her first boyfriend. I remember she was sulking; she resented having to be with us, away from him on a family vacation. She would find any excuse to run to a phone booth and call him, and of course I was really jealous. When we came back to Rome we found that the boy had painted huge graffiti in Italian on a wall right across from where we lived. Big, bold letters in bright green, with a crown on the top. It said something like 'Welcome back, Princess' . . ."

Julian paused and in his American accent said, " '*Benetornota . . . princessa'?*"

" '*Bentornata, principessa,*' " Valeria corrected him.

"Thank you. Actually, in America to be called a princess is a bit of an insult. My parents were absolutely furious, but Maya thought it was the most romantic thing that had ever happened to her."

Valeria smiled.

"My father had to pay someone to repaint the entire wall, but the writing was still visible beneath the new coat of paint. That graffiti survived her. It was eerie: it was faint but it was there and it literally faced our front door, so that after the accident each time we left the apartment we couldn't avoid seeing it."

Julian gave another look at the photo.

"Wait, I'll forward it to you."

Valeria watched him fiddle with his phone, and after a few seconds she heard a *ping* land inside her handbag. The photo had bounced from his phone to hers. The exchange felt too rapid, too clinical.

She checked her phone and enlarged the image. Valeria lingered, studying Maya's slender body, her tanned legs, the Capri sandals, the short orange dress that revealed her thighs, the hair, bleached by the sun, that almost reached her waist. She looked powerful for her age. Or maybe it was just the intensity of her being alive.

———

Julian was also staring at the same photo on his screen. His mind went to that particular summer—their last—after which everything seemed to have come to its end.

There was nothing that could be saved afterward.

Not Nero, Maya's black-and-white cat, who slept every single night sprawled around her neck with a paw on her cheek, like a baby who needs physical contact in order to fall asleep. He sat for three days refusing to eat or move from the crumpled shirt and jeans Maya had left on her bed that very same day. Then he vanished and nobody had the energy to go looking for him. It was understood that he no longer wished to live with them and that he'd carried his own grief elsewhere.

Not the house on the beach in Connecticut, where they'd spent every summer as a family. Too much happiness, too much blaring light, too much white and blue and breeze, bare feet stomping on the wooden porch, laughter at the breakfast table. The blond fuzz on Maya's arms, her red bikini, the shape of her body against the waves. The house was sold to a family of rich Lebanese who offered to buy it with the furniture. Take it all—it's free! they were told. Let us get rid of it in one go! his mother said. Who could have lived with it anyway?

Not the marriage, even though his parents remained together, inexplicably, even after they left Rome and went back to the States (a chaotic move, packing their belongings in a mix of tears and fury, like fugitives running from a war).

Maybe they simply had no energy left to split up since they were so broken already and their apartment on the Upper West Side offered enough space for each of them to forget the existence of the other. He in one room or at the UN office, she in another room, often in bed. He coming home late, she drinking Scotch. It was immediately obvious to Julian and his younger brother, Sam, that their parents had fallen into a void from which they were not planning to come back. There were no more meals together, no fire going in the living room, no fresh air in the apartment. Just irredeemable sadness and silence. It didn't matter that there were two more children to be told what to do or what to wear once the summer turned into fall, because they were still alive (which seemed almost unfair). Couldn't they just walk to the supermarket across the street or call the takeout numbers stuck on the refrigerator?

———

Julian suddenly felt exhausted.

Nothing this woman could tell him would help to soothe what he felt every time he thought of his sister: the hole Maya had carved inside him by her loss would always be there; all he had to do was pronounce her name. There was no closure. He loathed that word. He was just about to say something so that he and Valeria could part, when she spoke again.

"The only one who had the guts to say that it was my fault to my face was your mother."

"My mother?"

"Yes. She came to see me one night, I guess a few days or weeks after the accident. I was alone in the apartment, and when I opened the door I saw this towering figure in a long raincoat. I think it was raining because her hair was damp. I'd never seen her before, but I immediately knew who she was."

"She never told me she had gone to see you," Julian said.

"She stepped in before I could say anything. I offered her a chair in the kitchen but she ignored me. I remember she walked around, taking everything in, checking out this crummy place, messy and unkempt, and then she said, 'So, is this where you live? In this shithole?' Then she turned to me and said, 'Soon you won't be living here anymore. I will call the police and I'll have you evicted. You have killed my daughter and you mustn't live here anymore.' Which of course didn't have any logic to it, but it still terrified me."

Valeria stopped for a moment to catch her breath.

"And then she said, 'You will have to pay for this—I'll have you arrested.' Nothing she said made any sense, but you know . . . she had just lost her daughter, she was"—Valeria wiped the sweat from her eyebrows— "delirious with pain, or maybe she was under the effect of some medication . . . but I let her speak, not just because she was so commanding but also because I could tell she needed to unleash her anger. I just sat on a chair, paralyzed, while she stood up, staring at me with those wide eyes. She's very beautiful, your mother. Very intimidating. And I said nothing. Absolutely nothing."

Valeria stopped. Something inside her suddenly gave in, as if her sternum had splintered like a rotten plank.

"And now that I'm here talking to you it just seems incredible—*absurd,* actually—that I hadn't gone to her first, right after the accident, to tell her how sorry I was. Instead I'd been hiding like a criminal. Wanting to be punished, but also exonerated. Whereas she had the guts to come find me, to hunt me down."

Julian sprang up from the sofa as if his seat were burning and disappeared into the next room. Valeria remained seated. It was okay if he needed to move away from her. She waited a few minutes until she felt a bit lighter, a bit more peaceful. Someone had told her that three deep, long breaths were enough to quiet the body. She tried to take them, and once she felt a reasonable amount of time had passed without Julian returning to the room, she decided he wanted her to leave. She picked up her coat and knocked gently on the bedroom door, which he had left slightly ajar.

He was sitting on the side of the bed, elbows on knees, holding his head between his hands. She wasn't sure whether he was crying.

She waited, but Julian didn't move.

She knew she hadn't been helpful, but she couldn't think of anything to say, or a better way to end their meeting.

"It's late. I'm going to go now."

Julian lifted his head.

"Wait."

"What?"

"Come here."

He placed his hand on the side of the bed.

Valeria sat next to him. They were very close now, their shoulders touching.

"I thought of you often," he said. "How it must've been for you. Afterward. You too were so young."

Suddenly Julian put his arm around her back and pulled her to his chest in a headlock. She felt his hand press on the nape of her head and inhaled the foreign smell of his skin. She tried to look at him, but all she could see was his neck, and part of his jaw. She wrapped her arms around him too.

They held each other, tighter now, without speaking. Valeria perceived that Julian's body was shaking lightly—that vibration again, of too much blood rushing under the skin.

"Is this okay?" Julian asked.

Valeria nodded, then she felt something lift. It was light, like a whoosh, an opening. Her eyes welled up.

"Yes," she said.

———

The phone rang.

The early-morning light was seeping through the curtains, illuminating the room with a whitish glow.

Julian opened his eyes. He had slept very deeply.

"Jules? Did I wake you?"

"No. . . ." He cleared his voice. "Actually yes, but it doesn't matter. My alarm will go off in ten minutes anyway."

"I had a very bad day. Your phone call this morning threw me off completely."

His mother's voice was lightly slurred. He calculated the time difference: it was late-night in New York, the end of another day of Scotch on the rocks.

"You never told me you went to see her," he said.

"Who?"

"Valeria said you went to her apartment one night, a few weeks after the accident."

"Who? Me?"

"Yes, you. Don't you remember doing that?"

"No."

"Really?"

"Vaguely."

"That's all?"

"I don't know. Well, all right, yes. It was a terrible place. Dirty. She looked very scared. I don't remember what we said. I was out of my mind, of course."

Julian sighed.

"Mom, please go to bed. It's late there."

"I can't. I can't stop thinking about this. Can't you see? It's like reopening a wound."

"I know. But perhaps we can move on."

"Where to? To the fucking grave?" his mother snapped. "I'm seventy-six, Jules, for Christ's sake!"

Julian looked out of the window. The April sky was trimmed with lavender. One thing that had never changed in Rome was the beauty of the light.

"It wasn't just us. It was hard for her too," he said quietly, almost to himself, as he opened the window and leaned over the sill. "Please, try to rest, Mom. I've got to go now—I need to get ready for work."

———

Piazza del Popolo was deserted, and magnificent in its symmetry. The obelisk at its center and the two identical churches, one on each side of Via del Corso, formed a perfect triangle. Julian walked across that empty space, over the shiny cobblestones that had just been washed by the street-cleaning truck.

The previous night he had offered to call an Uber for Valeria, but she insisted she'd rather walk home, despite the late hour. She would be fine; Rome was a safe city, she said, and she just needed to be by herself. They had parted peacefully, knowing some of the weight they were each carrying had been dislodged and they could be grateful to each other for that. He had watched her from the suite's window, a solitary figure turning the corner of the empty street. He'd probably never see her again—there was no need to.

The driver wasn't coming for fifteen minutes, so Julian had a little time to be on his own before going to the production office for yet another meeting with the casting director. He was looking over at the tall, ancient pines swaying in the breeze at the top of Villa Borghese, when a gigantic flock of starlings moved across the sky like a handful of confetti thrown in the air. There were so many of them, they were like a dark stain over the pink sky. The shape they formed kept changing, stretching and contracting as if they were a single organism. He remembered how this particular pattern of migrant birds was called a murmuration, because of the sound produced by hundreds of flapping wings.

Julian stared at the dazzling display of the birds' flight. Who is the guide that leads them wherever they are heading? he asked himself. There was so much shared information and interdependence in the dance they were doing—heading north, then east, opening up and shrinking again in a mysterious choreography—so that the birds never collided but seemed to connect with and protect one another. What an amazing image to put in a film, he thought, so powerful and uplifting.

Are we also like that, he thought, humans moving unknowingly in formation, moved by the same intention? Is there a shared brain that connects us all if we listen carefully to one another, an instinct that allows us to move in sync, without hurting one another, toward a safer place?

He had no idea. But that morning so much of what he

wasn't sure of seemed possible to him, as he stood still in the empty square, mesmerized, in that incredible sweetness of light.

From the corner of his eye he saw the car appear at the corner of Caffè Rosati. He waved a hand and started to walk toward it.

ACKNOWLEDGMENTS

First and foremost I'd like to express my gratitude to Robin Desser, brilliant editor and friend, whose resilience and work on this book have been extraordinary. Thank you to my agents, the wonderful Nicole Aragi for her support and advice, and Giulia Pietrosanti for her insightful understanding. Thanks to everyone at Pantheon Books: you people are the best, with a special thank-you to Annie Bishai. I thank all the many people—dear friends and writers—who read early versions of these stories for their precious feedback: Jhumpa Lahiri, Chiara Barzini, Elizabeth Geoghan, Tiziana Lo Porto, Matthew Thomas, Richard Spera, Kathy and Michael Fitzgerald, Emma Campbell, and Camilla Paternò. Thank you, Zina, I owe you a lot.

A particular thank-you to Nick Reading and Chris Payne; they know why.

I also would like to acknowledge the brilliant books *H Is for Hawk* by Helen Macdonald and *The Pilgrim Hawk* by Glenway Wescott, both of which provided essential inspiration for the story "There Might Be Blood."

My deepest gratitude goes to the Sangam House writers' residency program at the CMI Institute in Chennai, for the peaceful time it granted me as a writer-in-residence.

THE OTHER LANGUAGE

A teenage girl encounters the shocks of first love at the height of the summer holidays in Greece. A young film-maker celebrates her first moment of recognition by impulsively buying a Chanel dress she can barely afford. Both halves of a longstanding couple fall in love with others and shed their marriage in the space of a morning. In all of these sparkling stories, characters take risks, confront fears, and step outside their boundaries into new destinies. Tracing the contours of the modern Italian diaspora, Francesca Marciano takes us from Venetian film festivals to the islands off Tanzania to a classical dance community in southern India. These stories shine with keen insights and surprising twists. Driven by Marciano's vivid takes on love and betrayal, politics and travel, and the awakenings of childhood, *The Other Language* is a tour de force that illuminates both the joys and ironies of self-reinvention.

Fiction

THE END OF MANNERS

Maria Galante and Imo Glass are on assignment in Afghanistan: outgoing Imo to interview girls who have attempted suicide to avoid forced marriage to older men, and shy, perfectionist Maria to photograph them. But in a culture in which women shroud their faces and suicide is a grave taboo, to photograph these women puts everyone in danger. Before the assignment is over, Maria is forced to decide if it's more important to succeed at her work—and please Imo—or to follow her own moral compass. *The End of Manners* is a story of friendship and loyalty, of the transformative power of journeying outside oneself into the wider world.

Fiction

CASA ROSSA

A crumbling farmhouse in Puglia, Casa Rossa was bought by Alina Strada's grandfather at a time when no one else wanted it. As Alina now prepares it for sale, she endeavors to recover the memories it still harbors—in particular of three women whose passions indelibly shaped her family's dark past. There's grandmother Renee, whose love of novelty won over everything else. Alina's mother, Alba, whose marriage to a screenwriter inspired both great art and unbearable sadness. And Isabella, Alina's sister, whose fervent politics drove her to ever-escalating betrayals. Moving from Jazz Age Paris to 1950s Rome to modern-day New York but returning always to the uncompromising beauty of Italy's south, *Casa Rossa* is a story of how loves and losses, secrets and lies resonate across the generations.

Fiction

RULES OF THE WILD
A Novel of Africa

Romantic, often resonantly ironic, moving, and wise, *Rules of the Wild* transports us to a landscape of unsurpassed beauty even as it gives us a sharp-eyed portrait of a closely knit tribe of cultural outsiders: the expatriates living in Kenya today. Challenged by race, class, and a longing for home, here are "safari boys" and samaritans, reporters bent on their own fame, and travelers who care deeply about elephants but not at all about the people of Africa. They all know each other. They meet at dinner parties, sleep with each other, and argue about politics and the best way to negotiate their existence in a place where they don't really belong. *Rules of the Wild* explores unforgettably our infinite desire for a perfect elsewhere, for love and a place to call home.

Fiction

Printed in the United States
by Baker & Taylor Publisher Services